"A true storyteller. . . . Martin Cruz Smith is
literate and exciting—think Joseph Conrad
on amphetamines."
—*Newsweek*

ACCLAIM FOR MARTIN CRUZ SMITH
AND ARKADY RENKO

"[Smith] takes what in essence is a police procedural and
elevates it to the level of absorbing fiction."

—*Los Angeles Times*

"A continuing adventure that in terms of popular fiction is
surely a work of art."

—*The Washington Post*

"Martin Cruz Smith knows his Russia. Every page reeks of
Moscow: dirty snow, the stink of cigarette and vodka fumes, the
cynicism and tasteless opulence of the mafia, the all-pervasive
corruption."

—*The Economist*

"Smith's gift for tart, succinct description creates a poisonous
political backdrop, one that makes his characters' survival skills
as important as any of their other attributes. [This is] one top-
flight series, still sharply honed, none the worse for wear."

—*The New York Times*

"There are few thriller practitioners indeed who can weld a
story to a graceful chassis of literature and send it barreling
away at top speed. Martin Cruz Smith is one of them."

—*The Buffalo News*

"As always, Smith elevates a police procedural story to a taste
of Russia, a glass of vodka poured quivering to the brim."

—Associated Press

Praise for *THREE STATIONS*

"Smith's Russian novels [have risen] to the level of social criticism, which great crime fiction has always done well. Like the luminaries of the genre, Smith is at heart a deeply moral writer, and beneath his wry, cynical tone you can feel his authorial anger twitching a safe distance away. Paired with what reads deceptively like a native's knowledge of Russia, it makes for a potent brew."

—*The New York Times Book Review*

"Smith's point hits its mark with requisite force. You can replace ideology, philosophy and people at the top, but basic human behavior—especially the worst of it—is embedded so deeply into psychological fabric that the same battles are waged even when the monsters keep shifting shapes. And Renko, like his detective siblings in crime, will remain to fight these monsters, no matter what sort of abyss they must look into, and which looks into them."

—*Los Angeles Times*

"Smith has made his career from all this [drama], and he does it extremely well. But what is the allure in depicting (and reading about) a society that is so screwed up? Perhaps it's because to fail in such a place becomes a moral victory. . . . Or maybe it's simply because Russia—the way it allegedly is now—makes us look good. Whatever it is, we evidently can't get enough of this ongoing story."

—*The Washington Post*

"Clear some room at the top of the bestseller list. Moscow Detective Arkady Renko is back in the bookstore."

—*St. Louis Post-Dispatch*

"Carefully crafted, cleverly designed and always riveting."

—*Providence Journal-Bulletin*

"By the time *Three Stations'* intertwining story strands wind tightly together, a reader has come to care about or marvel at the book's various characters as much as (it's clear) their author does."

—*San Francisco Chronicle*

"Martin Cruz Smith's latest and arguably best novel is a roller-coaster ride through the dark underbelly of present-day Russia. . . . Intact are the dark humor, intelligence, and power of observation that have made Renko the compelling literary figure he's been for decades."

—*Christian Science Monitor*

"The Renko series can be read as a critique of the political and social history of the Soviet Union and Russia, and is a great example of how crime fiction can explore just about anything as long as there's a crime involved and someone attempts to solve it. Students of modern Russia could benefit from following Renko around and seeing the country the way he sees it."

—*The Oregonian*

"Smith is a first-rate popular novelist, and this is one of his best books: tightly plotted, well constructed, with a host of memorable secondary characters. . . . Smith is always an inventive storyteller, and he brings this setting vividly to life."

—*Cleveland Plain Dealer*

"No one beats Cruz Smith at portraying the hopelessness of modern life while also showing how sometimes it is cynicism that keeps our humanity alive."

—*Booklist*

This title is also available from Simon & Schuster Audio and as an eBook

THREE STATIONS

AN ARKADY RENKO NOVEL

MARTIN CRUZ SMITH

G

GALLERY BOOKS

NEW YORK   LONDON   TORONTO   SYDNEY   NEW DELHI

Gallery Books
A Division of Simon & Schuster, Inc.
1230 Avenue of the Americas
New York, NY 10020

First Gallery Books trade paperback edition September 2011

GALLERY BOOKS and colophon are registered trademarks of
Simon & Schuster, Inc.

For information about special discounts for bulk purchases, please
contact Simon & Schuster Special Sales at 1-866-506-1949 or
business@simonandschuster.com.

The Simon & Schuster Speakers Bureau can bring authors to your live event. For
more information or to book an event, contact the Simon & Schuster Speakers
Bureau at 1-866-248-3049 or visit our website at www.simonspeakers.com.

Designed by Nancy Singer

Manufactured in the United States of America

10 9 8 7 6 5 4 3 2 1

The Library of Congress has catalogued the hardcover edition as follows:

Smith, Martin Cruz.
Three stations : an Arkady Renko novel / Martin Cruz Smith.
—1st Simon & Schuster hardcover ed.
     p. cm.
1. Renko, Arkady (Fictitious character)—Fiction. 2. Police—Russia
(Federation)—Moscow—Fiction. 3. Moscow (Russia)—Fiction.
4. Kidnapping—Fiction. I. Title.
PS3569.M5377T57 2010
813'.54—dc22   2010019996

ISBN 978-0-7432-7675-7
ISBN 978-1-4391-9992-3 (ebook)

FOR EM

MORE THAN EVER

THREE★STATIONS

1

The summer night swam by. Villages, ripening fields, derelict churches flowed and mixed with Maya's dreams.

She tried to stay awake but sometimes her eyelids had their way. Sometimes the girl dreamt of the train's first-class passengers tucked away asleep in their compartments.

Hard class had no compartments. "Hard class" was a dormitory coach where a few lamps were still lit and snoring, muffled sex, body odor and domestic quarrels were shared by all. Some passengers had been on the train for days and the fatigue of close quarters had set in. A round-the-clock card game among oil riggers soured and turned to resentment and accusations. A Gypsy went from berth to berth hawking the same shawls in a whisper. University students traveling on the cheap were deep in the realm of their headphones. A priest brushed cake crumbs from his beard. Most of the passengers were as nondescript as boiled cabbage. An inebriated soldier wandered up and down the corridor.

Still Maya preferred the rough sociability of hard class to traveling first class. Here she fit in. She was fifteen years old, a stick figure in torn jeans and a bomber jacket the texture of cardboard, her hair dyed a fiery red. One canvas bag held her earthly possessions, the other hid her baby girl of three weeks, tightly swaddled and lulled by the rocking of the train. The last thing Maya needed was to be trapped in a compartment under the scrutiny of snobs. Not that she could have afforded first class anyway.

After all, a train was just a communal apartment on rails, Maya decided. She was used to that. Most of the men stripped to warm-up pants, undershirts and slippers for the duration; she watched for any who had not because a shirt with long sleeves might conceal the tattoos of someone sent to bring her back. Playing it safe, she had chosen an otherwise empty berth. She talked to none of the other passengers and none noticed that the baby was on board.

Maya enjoyed creating stories about new people, but now her imagination was caught up with the baby, who was both a stranger and part of herself. The baby was, in fact, the most mysterious person she had ever met. All she knew was that her baby was perfect, translucent, unflawed.

The baby stirred and Maya went to the vestibule at the end of the car. There, half open to the wind and clatter of the train, she nursed the baby and indulged in a cigarette. Maya had been drug-free for seven months.

A full moon kept pace. From the tracks spread a sea of wheat, water tanks, a silhouette of a shipwrecked harvester. Six more hours to Moscow. The baby's eyes regarded her solemnly. Returning the gaze, Maya was so hypnotized that she did not hear the soldier join her in the vestibule until the sliding door closed behind him and he said smoking was bad for the baby. His voice was a jolt, a connection with reality.

He removed the cigarette from her mouth and snapped it out the vestibule window.

Maya took the baby from her breast and covered herself.

The soldier asked if the baby was in the way. He thought it was. So he told Maya to put the baby down. She held on, although he slid his hand inside her jacket and squeezed her breast hard enough to draw milk. His voice cracked when he told her what else he wanted her to do. But first she had to put the baby down. If she didn't, he would throw the baby off the train.

It took a second for Maya to process his words. If she screamed, could anyone hear her? If she fought, would he toss the baby like an unwanted package? She saw it covered with leaves, never to be found. All she knew was that it was her fault. Who was she to have such a beautiful baby?

Before she could put the baby down, the vestibule door opened. A large figure in gray stepped out, gathered the soldier's hair with the grip of a butcher and laid a knife across his neck. It was the babushka who had been suffering the crumbs of the priest. The old woman told the soldier she would geld him next time they met and gave him a vigorous kick as a demonstration of sincerity. He could not get to the next car fast enough.

When Maya and the baby returned to their berth, the babushka brought tea from the samovar and watched over them. Her name was Helena Ivanova but she said that everyone up and down the line called her Auntie Lena.

Worn-out, Maya finally allowed herself to plunge into true sleep, down a dark slope that promised oblivion.

When Maya next opened her eyes sunlight flooded the coach. The train was at a platform and the dominant sound was flies circling in the warm air. The fullness in her breasts was urgent. Her wristwatch said 7:05. The train was expected to arrive at six-thirty. There was no sign of Auntie Lena. Both baskets were gone.

Maya rose and walked unsteadily down the corridor. All the other passengers—the boisterous oil riggers, the university boys, the Gypsy and the priest—were gone. Auntie Lena was gone. Maya was the only person on the train.

Maya stepped onto the platform and fought her way through early-morning passengers boarding a train on the opposite side. People stared. A porter let his baggage cart coast into her shin. The ticket takers at the gate didn't remember anyone resembling Auntie Lena and the baby. It was a preposterous question from a ridiculous-looking girl.

People in the platform area were making good-byes and hundreds circulated around kiosks and shops selling cigarettes, CDs and slices of pizza. A thousand more sat in the haze of a waiting room. Some were going to the wilds of Siberia, some all the way to the Pacific and some were just waiting.

But the baby was gone.

2

Victor Orlov stood in a shower stall, his head bowed and his eyes shut while an orderly clad in a surgical mask, goggles, rubber apron and rubber gauntlets poured disinfectant on Victor's head until it dripped from his nose and four-day stubble, ran down his sunken stomach and naked ass and pooled between his feet. He looked like a wet, shivering ape with patches of body hair, black bruises and toenails thick as horn.

The station medic had been called "Swan" for a long time for his long neck. Having been a pickpocket and snitch, he was proud that he had worked his way to a position of responsibility and opportunity.

"I called as soon as Sergeant Orlov came in. I said to myself, call Senior Investigator Renko. He'd want to know."

"You did the right thing," Arkady said.

As the candle burned it released a florid, slightly rotten odor.

"We do what we can. So, is our old friend Victor using anything new, anything besides alcohol? Heroin, methadone, antifreeze?"

"Alcohol. He's from the old school."

"Well, the disinfectant will kill body lice, bacteria, microbes, fungi and spores. That's a bonus. Your friend's insides I can't do anything about. His blood pressure is low, but that's to be expected. His eyes are dilated, but there are no signs of head trauma. He's just detoxing. I gave him Valium and an injection of B_1 to calm him down. We should keep him here for observation."

"In a drunk tank?"

"We prefer 'sobriety station.'"

"Not if he can walk." Arkady held up a plastic bag with a change of clothes.

The orderly in the shower stall unreeled a hose and opened it full force. Victor took a step back as water drummed on his chest. The orderly circled him, hosing Victor from every angle.

It was not easy to be arrested for drunkenness. It was difficult to distinguish drunkenness from, say, sharing a bottle with friends, jolly times, sad times, saint's day, women's day, the urge to nap, the need to hold up a wall, the need to piss on the wall. It was hard to stand out as legitimately drunk when the bar was set so high. The consequences, however, could be dire. The fine was insignificant but family and colleagues would be informed—in Victor's case that would be his commander, who had already threatened to drop him a grade. Worse, multiple offenders had to spend two weeks in jail. Policemen did not thrive in jail.

A digital clock on the wall flipped to 2400.

Midnight. Victor was four hours late for his shift.

Arkady gathered his clothes from a dimly lit recovery area, moving among the beds of sedated men and urine-soaked sheets. The legs of the beds were sawed off to allow for falls. All the figures were still except for one who twisted against restraining belts and urgently whispered to Arkady, "I am God, God is shit, I am shit, God is shit, God is dog, I am God," over and over.

"You see, we get all types," Swan said. He had Victor's ID, keys, cell phone and handgun waiting when Arkady returned to the desk.

They dried and dressed Victor, trying to keep him from unraveling.

"He's not registered, right?" Arkady just wanted to check.

"He was never here."

Arkady laid fifty dollars on the desk and maneuvered Victor toward the door.

"I am God!" said the voice from the bed.

God is drunk, Arkady thought.

Arkady drove Victor's Lada because his own Zhiguli was in the shop awaiting a new gearbox and Victor had lost his license for drunk driving. It didn't matter that Victor had been washed and wore a change of clothes, the smell of vodka came off him like heat from a stove and Arkady cranked a window open for fresh air. The short nights of summer had begun, nothing like the white nights of St. Petersburg but enough to make sleep difficult and aggravate relationships. The police radio maintained a constant squawk.

Arkady handed Victor the walkie-talkie. "Call in. Let Petrovka know that you're on duty." Petrovka was shorthand for militia headquarters on Petrovka Street.

"Who cares? I'm fucked."

But Victor pulled himself together to call the dispatcher. Miraculously no one in his district had been murdered, raped or assaulted all evening.

"Bunch of fairies. Do I have my gun?"

"Yes. We'd hate to see that fall into the wrong hands."

Arkady thought Victor was nodding off but the detective muttered, "Life would be wonderful without vodka, but since the world is not wonderful, people need vodka. Vodka is in our

DNA. That's a fact. The thing is, Russians are perfectionists. That's our curse. It makes for great chess players and ballerinas and turns the rest of us into jealous inebriates. The question is not why don't I drink less, it's why don't you drink more?"

"You're welcome."

"That's what I meant. Thank you."

Other cars, beefed-up foreign monsters, roared up behind them but didn't tailgate for long. The Lada's exhaust pipe and muffler hung low and occasionally dragged a rooster tail of sparks, fair warning to keep a safe distance.

If the Lada was a wreck, so were the men in it, Arkady thought. He caught a glimpse of himself in the rearview mirror. Who was this graying stranger who rose from his bed, usurped his clothes and occupied his chair at the prosecutor's office?

Victor said, "I read in the paper about two dolphins trying to drown a man in Greece or someplace. You always hear about noble dolphins saving someone from drowning. Not this time; they were pushing him out to sea. I asked myself what was different about this poor bastard. It turned out he was Russian, naturally, and maybe a little drunk. Why does the reverse of the normal always happen to us? Maybe the dolphins had rescued him a dozen times before. Enough was enough. What do you think?"

"Maybe we should make it official," Arkady said.

"Make what official?"

"Russia is upside down."

Arkady was neither up nor down. He was an investigator who investigated nothing. The prosecutor made sure Arkady followed orders by giving him none to defy. No investigations meant no runaway investigations. Arkady was ignored, welcome to spend his time reading novels or arranging flowers.

Although he had time he hadn't spent it with Zhenya. At fifteen the boy was at the peak of sullen adolescence. Was Zhenya absent from school? Arkady had no say. His status with the boy was not official. All he could offer Zhenya was a clean place to spend the night. Arkady might not see him for a week and then by chance spot Zhenya in his other, secretive life trudging along in a hooded sweatshirt with a street gang. If Arkady approached, Zhenya froze him with a look.

The director of the children's shelter that Zhenya originally came from claimed that the boy and Arkady had a special relationship. Zhenya's father had shot Arkady. If that wasn't special, what was?

The day before, friends brought champagne and cake to celebrate Arkady's birthday, and then gave such rueful, eloquent speeches about the cost of integrity that the women cried. Some of the drunker men too, and Arkady had to go from person to person and reassure them that he was not dead.

He had written a letter of resignation.

As of noon today I resign my position in the Prosecution Service of the Russian Republic. Arkady Kyrilovich Renko, Senior Investigator of Important Cases.

But to afford Zurin so much satisfaction was unbearable. Arkady had burned the letter in an ashtray.

And the days marched on.

Arkady had a new neighbor across the hall, a young woman who was out all hours and sometimes needed help finding her latchkey in her voluminous bag. A journalist young enough to burn the candle at both ends. One night she showed up at his door with a black eye and a boyfriend in hot pursuit. The light on the landing was out, as usual, and Arkady did not get a good look at his face. However, the man could see Arkady in the open doorway, gun in hand, and vanished down the stairs in bounds.

"I'm fine. It was nothing," Anya said. "Really, thank you so much, you're the hero of the hour. I must look a mess."

"Who was it?"

"A friend."

"That was a friend?"

"Yes."

"Are you going to report this to the militia?"

"The militia? You must be kidding. Oh, you must be the investigator in the building. I heard about you," she said. "I take back any insinuation about the honesty and integrity of our brave men in their battle against the criminal element in our society."

He heard her whooping and laughing as soon as she was in her apartment.

The following night she knocked on Arkady's door and saw the bottles and plates of his birthday celebration scattered around the living room.

"A party?"

"It wasn't the Sack of Rome, just a few friends."

"Next time let me know." From her bag she gave him two tins of Osetra caviar, 125 grams each, together worth almost a thousand dollars.

"I can't."

"We're even. I get these all the time and I hate caviar. Where's the woman who lived here?"

"She left."

"Are you sure you didn't chop her into small pieces and mail her around the country? Just joking. You scared the shit out of my friend. Served him right."

Her name was Anya Rudikova. Oddly enough, he saw her a week later on television, black eye and all, discussing violence in film with the objectivity of a sociologist.

The radio dispatcher called and Arkady picked up on Victor's behalf.

"Orlov."

The dispatcher was cautious. She demanded to know whether he was fit for duty.

"Yes," Arkady said.

"Because when you called earlier you didn't sound so good. People are talking about you."

"Fuck them."

"Well, you do sound better. Can you handle an overdose? The ambulances are running late."

"Where?"

While Arkady listened he executed a satisfying U-turn in the face of oncoming traffic.

What tourist maps called Komsomol Square, the people of Moscow called Three Stations for the railway terminals gathered there. Plus the converging forces of two Metro lines and ten lanes of traffic. Passengers pushed their way like badly organized armies through street vendors selling flowers, embroidered shirts, shirts with Putin, shirts with Che, CDs, DVDs, fur hats, posters, nesting dolls, war medals and Soviet kitsch.

During the day Three Stations was in constant motion, a Circus Maximus with cars. At night, however, when the crowds were gone and the square was floodlit and gauzy with insects, Arkady felt that the stations were as exotic as opera sets. Leningrad Station was a Venetian palace, Kazansky Station was an Oriental mosque and Yaroslavl Station wore a clown's face and cap. The night revealed a population that the daytime bustle had obscured: pickpockets, flyboys handing out directions to strip clubs and slot arcades, gangs of street kids looking for the wounded, the slow, the easy mark. Men with vague intentions idled in small groups, beers in hand, watching prostitutes grind by. The women walked with a predatory eye and looked as likely to eat their clients as have sex with them.

Drunks were everywhere, but hard to see because they were

as gray as the pavement they sprawled on. They were bandaged or bloody or on crutches like casualties of war. Every doorway had a resident or two; they might be homeless but Three Stations was their roost. A beggar with broad shoulders and withered legs propelled his cart past a Gypsy who absentmindedly pulled out her baby and her breast. At Three Stations the crippled, outcast and usually hidden members of society gathered like the Court of Miracles only without the miracles.

Arkady jumped the curb at Yaroslavl Station and rolled across a small plaza to a workers' trailer that had stood in place so long its tires had deflated.

He asked Victor, "Do you want to stay in the car? I can cover for you."

"Duty calls. Someone may be pissing on my crime scene. Piss on a man's crime scene and you piss on the man himself."

Workers' trailers provided basic on-site accommodations: four bunk beds and a stove, but no toilet, shower or a/c. They baked in the summer and froze in the winter and from the outside the only concessions to human habitation was a sliding window and a door. After all, the workers were generally migrant labor from Central Asia. Tajiks, Uzbeks, Kirks, Kazakhs, although Russians tended to call them all Tajiks.

Russians were the actors, Tajiks the necessary but unseen stagehands who did the work too miserable or too dangerous for any local boy to consider.

Victor and Arkady were admitted by a railway police captain named Kol. The captain was cutting a raw onion and eating the slices against a summer cold. He wiped away tears.

"A lot of fuss for a dead whore."

The trailer's wiring had been ripped out but an extension cord entered through a window and ran to the ceiling hook, where a bare lightbulb cast a watery glow. The back of the trailer resembled the bottom of a trash barrel: hamburger wrappers, empty soda cans, broken glass and, on a lower bunk, a woman faceup and eyes open on a dirty mattress. Arkady guessed that she was eighteen or nineteen years old, fair-skinned. Soft brown hair and light blue eyes. She wore a cheap quilted jacket trimmed in synthetic "fur." One arm was raised as if making a toast. The other was tucked into her waist.

From the waist down, she was nude, legs crossed, and on the inside of her left hip the tattoo of a butterfly, a favorite motif among prostitutes. A half-empty liter of vodka stood on the floor next to a denim skirt, underpants and shiny high-heeled boots. Arkady would have covered her but the rule was no touching until the forensic technicians had finished.

Scattered on the mattress were a black patent-leather handbag, lipstick, rouge, hairbrush, douche, toothpaste and toothbrush, tissue, pepper spray and an open bottle of aspirin. Yellow powder spilled from the bottle. What Arkady did not find was an ID.

Kol took a position inside the trailer door. Hash and heroin flowed through Three Stations and relations between the militia and railway police was a truce between thieves.

Victor asked, "Who found the body?"

The captain said, "I don't know. We got a call from someone passing through."

"How many is that?"

"People passing through Three Stations on an average day? About a million. I don't remember every face."

"Do you remember her?"

"No, that tattoo I'd remember." Kol couldn't take his eyes off it.

Arkady asked, "Who put the trailer here?"

"How should I know?"

"Nice knife."

"It's sharp enough."

Apart from the fact that the woman was dead, she seemed

in good health. Arkady saw no obvious cuts or bruises. From her temperature, muscle tone and the absence of lividity—the purple stripes of pooled blood—he guessed that she was dead no more than two hours. He played the beam of a penlight on blue irises gone slack. There was no bleeding in the corneas or any other indication of head trauma. No roseate nose, raw cheeks or needle tracks. Her forearms and hands presented no defensive wounds or scraped knuckles and there was grime but no scratched tissue under her fingernails. It was as if she had slept through her death.

Victor came to life; murder always did that for him. The forensics van would generate photographs he could circulate among streetwalkers, kiosk clerks and other nighttime regulars. Arkady took a short stroll around the trailer looking for items of clothing that might have been dropped, but the streetlamps in back of the square were so few and so dim it was like wading through water. The apartment building opposite Yaroslavl Station could have been a distant planet. Even prostitutes hesitated to enter some corners.

Of course, there were prostitutes and prostitutes. Exotic beauties at expensive clubs like Night Flight or the Nijinsky demanded $1,000 a night. At the bar of the Savoy Hotel, $750. Room service at the National Hotel, $300. An all-night Thai masseuse, $150. Oral sex in Lubyanka Square, $10. Three Stations, $5. It was a wonder the captain hadn't scraped her up with a shovel.

Victor took a call on the car phone, saying only, "Yes . . . yes . . . yes" until he clicked off.

"Petrovka demands to know what I've got. Homicide, suicide, accident, overdose or natural causes? If I don't have evidence of deliberate foul play, they want me to move on. The ambulance will come when it comes. Some oligarch lost his little dog in a garage. Petrovka wants me to go there, get on my hands and knees and help find the little puppy. If I find it first I will twist its furry head off."

"You'd leave before the technicians get here?"

"If she's an accident or natural causes, there won't be any forensic technicians or autopsy. They'll collect her, and if she goes unclaimed for a week, she'll go to the medical school or up in smoke." Victor squinted to get a thought in focus. "All I know is that she was dealing with a perverse individual. Nobody leaves half a liter of good vodka with the cap off."

"Your point being . . . ?"

"He could afford another bottle. He had money."

"And this wealthy individual chose to have sex on a dirty mattress in a trailer?"

"It wasn't in the street. And then there's the butterfly tattoo. That's an identification plus."

Captain Kol was slicing the onion with his eyes fixed on the girl when he exploded with "Fuck!" He had cut himself and blood ran from his onion to his elbow. "Shit!"

"No bleeding, pissing or picking your nose around my crime scene." Victor launched the captain out of the trailer. "Cretin!"

She didn't look like a homicide, suicide or OD to Arkady. No sedatives, no needle tracks or peg teeth of a methadone user.

"What's that?" Victor noticed the open aspirin bottle and yellow powder.

"We'll have to wait for the lab to tell us."

Victor licked a gloved fingertip, dipped it in the bottle and came up with a dab of powder that he smelled, tasted and spat out like a wine expert dismissing an inferior Bordeaux.

"Clonidine. Blood pressure pills. Want a taste?"

"I'll take your word for it."

"A cocktail of clonidine and vodka would drop Rambo in his tracks." Victor warmed to the thought. "Rambo would wake up with no money, no clothes, no bow and arrow, and now we have a case. Madame Butterfly here had the criminal intention and the means of rendering some innocent man unconscious and robbing him."

Arkady shook his head. "'Madame Butterfly'?"

"Well, we have to call her something. I'm not going to spend the night saying 'the deceased.'"

"Anything but Butterfly."

"Okay. There are so many Russian prostitutes in Italy that the new word for whore there is 'Natasha.'"

Arkady said, "That would presume she was a prostitute. It would affect our attitude."

"Never mind the trailer, the sex, the drugs. Do you prefer Princess Anastasia? Olga? There's a name you trust."

"What does she look like?"

Victor brushed a fly from her ear. "To me she looks like—apart from the makeup and skimpy clothing—a nice country girl."

"I agree. Olga."

"Good. I'm worn-out and we've hardly started."

"The problem is that Olga screwed up with the knockout drops. Or this guy saw what she was up to and switched glasses when her back was turned. Maybe he spiked her glass even more. She passed out. He robbed her and took off."

"Another problem," Arkady said. "There are no glasses—"

"We can always get new glasses and rub a little sleep dust on her lips. Otherwise, they'll bag our Olga and dump her and no one will notice or care. She'll sink without a fucking ripple. I'm not saying we should come to any conclusions, just keep an open mind."

There was an almost gawky quality to the girl, as if she had not yet grown into her long legs. Her knees were dirty but not scabbed. Arkady wondered what she would look like if her face were washed.

Victor studied the vodka bottle. Half empty or half full, the bottle had a silvery allure. Neither man had touched it for fear of smearing prints. Arkady heard the detective's dry swallow.

"You know what's tragic about all the money floating around?" Victor said.

"What's tragic?"

"A bottle of vodka used to cost ten rubles, just the right sum for three people to share. Not too much, not too little. That was how you met people and made friends. Now they have money they got selfish. Nobody shares. It's torn apart the fabric of society." Victor raised his head. "There's not a scratch on her. You fished me out of the drunk tank for nothing."

"Probably."

Victor said, "Why don't you come with me to the garage? The dog's name is Fuck Off."

"We need a witness or, at the very least, her pimp. Fortunately the pimp is near."

"Where?"

Arkady ran his finger along the extension cord from the lightbulb to the window. "At the other end of this."

While Victor went out Arkady stayed in the trailer with the dead girl and the bottle of vodka. Contract killings aside, four out of every five violent crimes involved vodka. Vodka faithfully attended every human activity: seduction, matrimony, celebration and, definitely, murder.

Sometimes a scene told a story in dramatic terms: a kitchen table with so many beer and vodka bottles there was hardly room to set a glass, knives on the floor, blood smeared the length of the hall to two bodies, one crisscrossed with stab wounds and the other peppered with bullet holes. In comparison the trailer scene was a still life, horizontal, nothing left standing but the bottle.

Arkady was aware that he was missing something profoundly obvious, some basic contradiction. Now when he needed imagination all he could summon was Victor's story about the wayward swimmer and the dolphins. Arkady felt his own invisible dolphins pushing him out to sea and away from land.

He sat on the bunk opposite the dead girl. She had an oval Slavic face that was more soulful than that of Western women and her hair was not simply brown but a dove's mix of ash and brown. Her gaze was averted from the grossness of her pose. Pale bands on her fingers showed where rings had been removed, not forcibly; there was no bruising of the joints. He saw no sign on her of violence new or old, but given the choice between investigating the murder of a streetwalker or writing her off as a "death by natural causes," Petrovka would happily accept the proposition that a young woman in apparent good health had undressed, lain down for sex in a trailer and peacefully expired. Finis!

Arkady lifted the vodka bottle off the floor by its bottom edge and stopper. A circle of water marked the floor where the bottle had been. Then something fell from the bottom of the bottle to his feet and he picked up a silver plastic card that said in black script, *Your VIP pass to the Nijinsky Luxury Fair*. The reverse side had a bar code and *June 30–July 3, Club Nijinsky, Browsing begins at 8 p.m.*

June 30 was two hours ago. Arkady went to the window. Finding a witness among the furtive citizens of Three Stations promised to be a farce. In this particular place who would notice a prostitute practicing her trade? His eye ran to the apartment house across the plaza. Eight stories mainly of dark flats, but some with kitchen lights on or the hypnotic glow of television on the ceiling. The trailer door opened and Victor was back, saturnine and triumphant.

"You'll never guess."

"Surprise me," Arkady said.

"Okay. Our extension cord runs from here and goes directly to the railway police station. I saw our friend the captain through a window. He's got a bandage on his hand the size of a boxing glove. But the cord doesn't end there; it's connected to another long cord that's plugged into an outlet at the back of the militia station. Got it? We're the pimps. You don't look surprised."

3

So far as Zhenya was concerned, Yaroslavl Station offered just about everything: buffets, bookstore, kiddy corner, shops selling cigarette lighters, CDs and DVDs. A lounge for soldiers; men on leave traveled free. An escalator led to an upper waiting hall that featured a concert piano behind a red velvet rope.

He started on the main floor and watched for anyone willing to play a friendly game of chess on the folding board he had in his backpack. He was cautious; he always carried his ID and a commuter pass in case he was stopped. Although he was half hidden in a sweatshirt and hood, he stayed in the blind spots of ceiling cameras focused on him.

When he didn't see a likely opponent, Zhenya retreated to a bench on a quiet corridor off the upper hall and studied a pocket English-Russian dictionary. Bobby Fischer had learned Russian to read proper chess analysis; Zhenya was returning the favor. Zhenya concentrated on the talented word "draw," which described the inconclusive ending of a chess match. Or pulling, pouring, sketching, attracting, earning, opening or closing drapes and more.

With a click the door across from Zhenya opened. Inside, two militia officers and a girl sat at a metal table with a plastic pitcher of water, paper cups and a tape recorder. The senior officer was a woman, a major by the stars on her shoulder boards. A lieutenant tipped back in his chair.

The girl was about fifteen, Zhenya's age. Her eyes were blurred by tears, and since she had dyed her hair a neon red, she was exactly the type the militia liked to harass, but the major used a motherly tone.

"First necessary information and then the search. Everything will turn out fine. Maybe someone will find your lost baby before we're even done."

"I didn't lose her, she was stolen."

"So you said. We'll get into that."

"We're wasting time. Why aren't you looking for her?"

"My dear, we have a systematic approach that works well. This is a problematic case. You say that you don't have any photographs of the baby."

"A baby is a baby."

"Still it is a shame. A photograph is crucial in finding someone."

"Did you find them?" The girl pointed to the faces pinned to the wall, black-and-white photocopies of snapshots grainy from enlargement, taken indoors or out, of different ages and either sex but the people in them had one thing in common: they had disappeared.

"Sadly, no. But you have to help us."

"We can't hand over a baby to just anyone," the lieutenant said.

"Lieutenant . . ." As if to a naughty boy.

"Just playing with her head."

The major said, "Your train arrived more than an hour ago.

You should have come to us then. Time is critical in finding a child alive."

"We're wasting time now."

"Your full name?"

"Maya."

"That's all?"

"That's all."

"Are you married, Maya?"

"No."

"I see. Who is the father?"

"Someone I met, I suppose."

The lieutenant said, "Someone she met."

"I don't know." Still, woman-to-woman, the major seemed sympathetic.

"You're very young to have a baby. What grade are you in?"

"I graduated."

"You don't look it. Show me your ticket and papers, please."

"They were in my basket. I had two baskets, one for the baby and one for her things. She has a special blue blanket with yellow ducklings. All gone."

"A birth certificate?"

"Gone. I know the color of her eyes and her hair and birthmark. Things only a mother would know."

"Do you have any papers at all for you or the baby?"

"Stolen."

"Can your parents supply this information?"

"They're dead."

"So on paper this baby does not exist and on the train it was invisible. Is that what you're saying?"

The girl was silent.

"At what station did you board? Come now. You must know at what station you got on the train."

"Or when she disappeared."

"I told you. She was stolen while I was asleep. She was in a basket."

"And you blame this so-called Auntie Lena?"

"Have you heard of her? She said everyone knew her."

"No, I have never heard of such a person. Did you talk to anyone besides Auntie Lena?"

"No."

"Did anyone else see the baby?"

"No."

"Were you hiding the baby?"

The girl said nothing, although she felt the questions accelerate.

"What about the soldier?" the major asked.

"Sorry?"

"In your first version there was a soldier. You said you took your baby to the end of the car."

"For fresh air."

"For fresh air and out of view of the rest of the passengers?"

"Yes."

"And very private."

"I guess."

"And there you were joined by the soldier."

"Yes."

"You and the soldier and the invisible baby."

"Yes."

The girl saw where they were headed. It was like suddenly finding herself being dragged down a snake hole. She spaced out, and when she tuned back in, the major was speaking with an air of conclusion. ". . . a false alarm. Taking her age into account, her fantasy might not have malicious intent, but a dangerous fantasy it is because the terrorist threat is real. A full-bore hunt would have demanded scores of militia chasing the chimera of a stolen baby. There is no stolen baby because there was no baby to steal. No further action will be taken by the Search Department, except to remand for observation the juvenile who identifies herself only as Maya." The major turned off the recorder and added, "Sorry, dear. I never believed it from the start. No one would."

"Just tell me," the lieutenant said. "When you and the soldier went to the end of the car, did you give him a hand job or a blow job?"

Zhenya couldn't see what happened in the interview room. He heard shouts and the sound of water mixed with breaking glass. The door flew open as the lieutenant, soaked through, rushed the girl through the corridor, past the velvet rope and piano and down the escalator, holding her by the collar of her jacket so that her feet barely touched the floor. One moment he was lifting her into the air and the next she slipped clean out of her jacket and bolted through the waiting room.

The lieutenant pursued her, his knees pumping, suddenly a track star. In the lingering twilight the pavement was still active despite the hour. The lieutenant was nearly within reach when she darted behind a stack of parcels, between pensioners in wheelchairs, under a table of souvenirs and finally through an extended family of Chechens. Some devious shit, Zhenya thought. People cheered and applauded the girl's wild dash. Zhenya watched in awe.

"Cunt!" The officer pulled up lame and threw the girl's jacket. He limped in a circle to catch his breath, and by the time the cramp in his leg began to ease, the girl had disappeared. He didn't even know in which direction. Would it have been so hard for a citizen to stick out a foot and trip the little bitch? The arrogant shits of Moscow had, as usual, given the militia no help at all. For example, he went to collect the girl's jacket and it was gone.

★

It wasn't difficult for Zhenya to find the girl. Her red hair was hard to hide, and although she had found the underground connection to the Metro, he didn't think she was going far. He went through the contents of her jacket: reading glasses, a butane lighter, half a pack of "Russian Style" cigarettes and an envelope containing 1,500 rubles, the rough equivalent of sixty dollars, which Zhenya suspected was all the money she had in the world. No cell phone and no ID. Internal passports were issued at sixteen years. She was no older than he was.

The Metro was a grandiose Stalin-era hole in the ground a hundred meters deep, an air-raid shelter with ballroom chandeliers and escalators that clacked like wooden teeth. The girl was ten steps below him.

How crazy was she? The lieutenant aside, wouldn't a real mother have supplied all the information the major demanded? There would have been a proper search with bulletins, television appeals, adequate manpower and search dogs. Probably she was mentally unbalanced and "Baby" would turn out to be a lost pet.

Riders divided onto the platform or to the escalator to another, deeper subway line. Alone, the girl went to the far end of the platform and slipped down behind an octagonal column of limestone. Zhenya followed at a distance in a self-appointed, vaguely protective way. Over the train tunnel a digital clock began counting down from five minutes until the next train.

A mural in gilded tiles celebrated Soviet labor, and on the ceiling—for those with rubber necks—spread a gallery of patriots. The rush of air through tunnels seen and unseen and around the columns sounded like a respiratory system beneath the earth.

She was peeved as he came around the last column, as if her concentration had been broken. Or a private moment violated. To himself he said, "This is fucked."

Sitting cross-legged, the girl pressed a razor against her

wrist but not hard enough yet to pop the vein. Double-edged. She might have outraced the lieutenant minutes before. Now she looked catatonic. As she raised her eyes he understood that at any moment he could be standing in blood.

"Do you have my baby?"

"I can help," Zhenya said. He drew her leather jacket out of his backpack and showed her that the money and other contents were still in the jacket pockets, but she wouldn't take her eyes off his.

"You don't have my baby?"

"But I can help you. No one knows Three Stations better than me. I'm here all the time. Every day." He talked fast with his eye on the blade. "I'm just saying if you want, you know, I can help."

"You'll help me?"

"I think so."

"In exchange for what?"

"What do you mean?"

She let a pause build. "You know what I mean."

"No." Zhenya's face went red.

"It doesn't matter." Keeping the razor poised became tiresome and she let her arms relax. "Where are we?"

"The Metro under Three Stations. You've never been here before?"

"No. Why aren't you in school?"

"Bobby Fischer used to say school was a waste of time, that he never learned anything in school."

"Who is Bobby Fischer?"

"The greatest chess player in history."

She gave him a blank look. Zhenya had no experience with girls. They treated him as if he were invisible and he returned the favor. He didn't modulate his voice in public and he was a disaster at conversation, yet he thought he must have said something right, because she slid the razor into a cardboard sleeve and got to her feet. With the tinkling of chandeliers and a buffeting of air, a train entered the station along the near side of the platform. If she had asked, he could have told her to avoid cars marked with a red stripe because of cracks in the under-carriage. He knew all sorts of stuff.

She asked, "How old are you?"

"Sixteen." He added a year.

"Sure."

"My name is Zhenya Lysenko."

"Zhenya Lysenko, Zhenya Lysenko." She found the name uninspiring.

"What's yours?"

"Maya."

"Just Maya?"

"Maya."

"I saw you outrun the lieutenant. That's typical. You go to them for help and almost get arrested."

"I don't need them."

"Do you have family in Moscow?"

"No."

"Friends?"

"No."

A train arrived on the other side of the platform and the din of passengers made speech impossible. By the time the train closed its doors and drew away from the platform, Zhenya had added it up. All she had was him.

Zhenya and Maya pushed through the amorphous mass that was a Russian queue, past *biznesmen* whose business fit into a suitcase, Uzbek women swathed in color, babushkas draped in gray, soldiers on leave sucking their last beer dry. Most of the trains were *elektrichkas*, locals with overhead cables, but some were destined to cross mountains and deserts to exotic locales thousands of kilometers away. An express left Platform 3. Halfway across the station yard the train met heat waves, entered a lagoon of semaphores and signals, sank and disappeared. The Platform 3 conductor, an energetic woman in a blue uniform and running shoes, fanned herself with her signal paddle and thought that if the two teenagers coming her way had missed their train there was nothing she could do about it now.

Zhenya and Maya had switched. She wore his sweatshirt open but with the hood up to conceal her red hair and he, in turn, had pulled on her leather jacket, even though the sleeves rode high on his skinny forearms. Out the corner of his eye he admired the way Maya boldly marched up to the conductor.

"You're not the conductor who was here this morning."

"Of course not. Her shift is over."

"And this morning's trains?"

"Back in service. Why? Did you lose something?"

"Yes."

The conductor was sympathetic. "I'm sorry, dear. Anything you leave on a train is probably gone for good. I hope it had no sentimental value."

"I lost my baby."

The conductor looked from Maya to Zhenya and back.

"Are you serious? Have you been to the Search Department?"

"Yes. They don't believe me."

The conductor lost her breath all at once. "Good Lord, why not?"

"They want to know too much. I just want my baby. A girl three weeks old."

"Is this true?" the conductor asked Zhenya.

"She thinks it was stolen by someone called Auntie Lena."

"I never heard of her. What is your name, dear?"

"Maya."

"Are you married, Maya?"

"No."

"I understand. Who is the father?" The conductor gave Zhenya a significant glance.

Maya said, "Not a chance. I just met him."

The conductor thought for a moment before asking Zhenya, "Have you seen the baby?"

"No."

"Then I'm so sorry. It's a criminal matter if a baby has been abducted. The Search Department is the proper authority. I wish I could help."

"She has a faint birthmark on the back of her neck. Almost like a question mark. You have to lift her hair to see it."

Zhenya thrust a piece of paper into the conductor's hand. "This is my cell-phone number. Please call if you hear anything."

A man with a suitcase in one hand and a toddler in the other arrived at the platform to find that their train was gone. As the man slowed to a standstill the toddler slipped to the ground and cried.

Tears escaped from Maya's eyes. Worse, to her fury, was how her breasts ached.

Zhenya steered her off the platform. Now that the crying had begun, she couldn't stop, as if at that moment her baby were being wrested from her hands. Not sobbing but bent over and racked. Zhenya prided himself on his lack of emotion and it was frightening how her crying knotted his throat.

He said, "This is fucked, this is really fucked."

"My baby."

"I know an investigator in the prosecutor's office. He's a decent guy."

"No prosecutors, no police."

"Just talk to him. Whoever took the baby could have gone a hundred different ways. Two people can't cover them all."

"No police."

"He'll help privately."

The suggestion mystified her. "Why would he do that?"

"He's got nothing else to do."

By Kazansky Station was a two-story building with a militia sign so discreet it might have been a public toilet. Over the years Arkady had visited a dozen times to take a suspect for interrogation or to save a suspect from interrogation and the risers of the stairs were appropriately faced with cracked tiles that looked like broken teeth. He climbed the steps to a squad room with the residue of pizza boxes, grease boards, dusty photos of forgotten heroes, old bulletins curled into yellow scrolls, new bulletins in the wastebasket and desks marked by cigarette burns and coffee stains, much the way Arkady felt.

In a corner office Colonel Malenkov, sunburned and slathered with cream, was hanging a certificate on the wall. Every movement looked painful. His bald spot looked painful.

"Enough of fucking Crete and its fucking sun. It was full of Russians anyway."

The certificate stated that Colonel Leonid N. Malenkov had attended a "Tenth Annual International Conference on Counterterrorism." Similar certificates from Tunis, Amsterdam and Rome were already hung.

Arkady said, "They're tilted."

"They shift. It's the vibration from the trains. Sometimes the whole building shakes."

Arkady read the motto that appeared in English on each certificate: *Vigilance Keeps Us Free*. What does that mean?"

"Terrorists cooperate on a global level. We must do the same."

"Good. You can cooperate with me."

"You've got some brass."

"The dead girl in the trailer. She was in your precinct. Why didn't you respond to the dispatcher?"

Malenkov moved stiffly to his desk and settled gently on his chair. "Renko, you tried to have me up for running a prostitution ring. Fortunately the prosecutor didn't think you had a case. Justice was served and you went home to chew on your dick. Why would I talk to you?"

"You have no one else to talk to. This place is empty."

"That's right. They're all out on cases. Real cases."

"Do you mind if I smoke?"

"I wouldn't mind if you blow it out your ass. I can't believe you have the balls to walk in here."

"How would you like to do it again?"

"Do what?"

"Go through another investigation."

"You'd lose again."

"But it was expensive, wasn't it? As I remember, you had lawyers."

"Fucking leeches." Usually Malenkov employed physical threats; the sunburn had obviously affected him. "I heard you were in some kind of deep freeze."

"Yet here I am."

"What are you after? You're always after something."

"A little conversation."

"Well, you're a little ahead of yourself. An investigator only takes over when the detectives are done."

"It's not my case. I happened to be riding with Lieutenant Orlov when the call came in."

"The last time I saw Victor Orlov he couldn't piss straight enough to hit a barn."

"His aim has improved."

"Good. Then he ought to be able to handle a simple overdose."

"We're not certain that it was simple."

"One dead skank is pretty much like another."

Arkady handed his cell phone to Malenkov. Olga filled the screen. Death gave her a quiet that only made her youth more poignant. Arkady let the colonel's eyes have their fill.

Malenkov shrugged. "Okay, she was a pretty girl. Moscow is full of pretty girls."

"She wasn't in your string?"

"I don't know what you're talking about. A precinct commander doesn't have much contact with the general public unless they're murdered or torched."

"Torched? That happens often?"

"You know kids. Do you have any witnesses?"

"Sergeant Orlov is canvassing the area."

"From the freak show here? People here see cockroaches as big as dogs."

"She was found in a workers' trailer twenty-five meters from where we are right now. Extension cords run from the back of this station house to the trailer. It's your trailer."

Malenkov slid Arkady's cell phone back across the desk. "It's an abandoned trailer. Let me ask you, was this girl raped? Beaten? Did you see any 'unusual circumstances'?"

"Her underpants were taken and she was left on display. That sounds 'unusual' to me."

"Really? How unusual is it for a prostitute to remove her panties? As I remember, that's what they're paid to do. You say she was 'on display'? Some clients only want to watch. Girls arrive from the countryside every day to let them fuck, watch or whatever. We have a flood of them. They shoot up and overdose because they're not the brightest individuals in the world. So we don't waste time on ODs."

"You bury them as quickly as you can."

"Life is unfair. Why should death be any different?"

An audible shimmy ran through the building as two hundred tons of diesel locomotive approached on a near track. The certificate from Crete shifted, Rome trembled, Tunis leaned and Amsterdam followed suit. While Malenkov was occupied with adjusting them, Arkady scooped his cell phone into an envelope, taking care not to smear the colonel's fingerprints.

5

Zhenya didn't understand why Maya refused to go to the militia; this was one of those rare occasions when the police might do some good. There should be a manhunt and pictures of the baby shown on the news. How else to cover three major railway stations and their Metro connections? Instead, she insisted on begging for information from platform conductors, cleaning ladies and café staff while she refused to divulge her own name or where she came from. The more questions she asked the more suspicion she aroused.

When evening came they found themselves still in Yaroslavl Station, wading through row after row of sleeping figures. Carefully. Families could misinterpret the intent of a stranger hovering over their babies. The upstairs waiting room had a piano behind a velvet rope; Zhenya had never heard anyone play it. A peek into the luxury lounge found only Americans and potted plants.

When Maya began to stagger, Zhenya led her outside for

fresh air. At this hour Three Stations had the stillness of a circus when the show was over and tents were struck. Zhenya bought an apple at a twenty-four-hour kiosk and sliced it for Maya with a folding knife. Maya ate listlessly, mainly at his urging.

The kiosk was a vodka stop for prostitutes. Zhenya regarded them out of the corner of his eye and all he saw was an impression of lipstick smears, bruised flesh and net stockings. When pimps began to gravitate in Maya's direction, Zhenya led her toward the relative safety of a taxi rank.

Traffic in the square was five lanes each direction and the night resounded with the boom of foreign cars that seemed to rise out of the ground at full speed.

Maya pointed across the square to a giant Oriental gate, dark arches and a floodlit clock tower.

"Is that a station too?"

"Kazansky Station. I think we should call my friend."

"The policeman?"

"A prosecutor's investigator."

"No difference."

"He's been around a long time. He might have some ideas."

"Just tell me how to get across."

So much for Arkady, Zhenya thought.

He steered Maya to a pedestrian underpass that was a hundred meters of flickering lights and shuttered stalls. During the day the passage was an arcade of small shops that traded in phone cards, flowers, women's hose. The single stall without shutters was protected by two uniformed security guards dozing in their chairs.

Zhenya said, "We can come back when there are more people."

"I'm looking for my baby now. I didn't ask for help, you volunteered."

"Only a suggestion."

"What's the matter? Do you have enemies down here?"

Worse, Zhenya thought. Friends.

The waiting hall at Kazansky Station put Zhenya in mind of the nocturnal habitat at the zoo, a place where things stirred indistinctly and species were difficult to identify. Were these silhouettes hunchbacks or hikers with their packs? Was that ominous hulk a suitcase or a bear? Zhenya held his breath while Maya stumbled over the mega-luggage of vendors and the bare legs of slumbering tourists.

This was worse than insane, Zhenya decided, it was futile. He slipped behind a photo booth and tried to call Arkady at home. He waited ten rings before giving up because Arkady sometimes ignored the phone and message machine. Next, Zhenya tried Arkady's cell phone, which rang only twice before Maya snatched the phone away.

"I said no police."

"You'll never find the baby this way."

"Your first chance, you snuck away and called them."

"Just talk to him."

"No police, we agreed."

"He's not police."

"Police enough."

"Okay, it's your move."

"I'm going back to the other station. Anyway, it's not your problem." She unzipped Zhenya's sweatshirt and returned it to him. "Why do I trust strangers? I'm so stupid."

"How are you going to get by?"

"I'll get by. I know how to do that."

"You don't know Three Stations."

"I just took the tour."

"And you don't know your way around Moscow. It's twenty-four hours since you saw your baby. You don't need a search party, you need a time machine."

"That's not your problem, is it?"

She headed for the street, and when Zhenya tried to walk with her, she shook him off. His sense of honor demanded that he keep her in sight even if it meant tagging a humiliating distance behind her.

Maya took the pedestrian underpass. Harsh lights were welcome after the murk of the stations and she was reassured by the sight of a group of boys coming from the far end. She was surprised to see them out so late, but the fact that they were singing made her feel safe and she shot Zhenya a look that warned him off.

A tourist approached with the teenage boys. He was drunk and out of shape and he ran in slow motion, arms flailing like a marathoner down to his last gasp. Designer eyeglasses bounced on his nose. Tassels bounced on his shoes. The boys trotted alongside in dirty sneakers and salvaged clothes. Older boys tucked a cigarette behind an ear. One was actually a girl with fuzzy dreadlocks that swung from her cap. As they sang, the acoustics of the tunnel made sound seem as visible as rings of smoke.

"Beck in the Yuuessessaarr . . ."

The drunk had a task enough in staying upright. Blood matted his hair and dripped strawberry-colored stains on his polo shirt. When he saw the security guards he shouted over and over that he was registered at the Canadian embassy, as if that made a difference.

"Oww luggee yuuaarr . . ."

The guards were paid to protect one stall, nothing else, and the Canadian swept by in the grip of a boy old enough to cultivate a wispy mustache and the air of authority. A white scarf was around his neck and he carried the butt end of a billiard cue as a club. Maya kept walking as the procession approached; animals—dogs or boys—were more likely to chase anything that ran.

The Canadian tripped and fell. At once the boys swarmed

over him, removing his watch and stripping him of his visa, passport, credit cards and money. Maya seemed to get no more than a glance. She made it almost to the bottom of the stairs before the boy with the scarf slipped in front of her.

"Terrific hair."

Now she wished she had never dyed it.

He said, "I'm Yegor. What's your name?"

She didn't answer.

Yegor wasn't insulted. He was sixteen at least, a combination of baby fat and muscle, the proper build for a bully, and when she tried to step around him, he held the pool cue in her way.

"Where are you going?"

"Home."

"Where's home? I can take you."

She said, "My brother is meeting me."

"I'd like to meet him." Yegor pantomimed looking around.

"You won't like him."

"What's the matter with him? Too big? Too little? Maybe he's a fag?"

"He's waiting."

"I don't think so. What do you think, Boots?"

The girl with dreadlocks said, "I don't think there's a brother."

"I agree with Boots. I don't think there's a brother and I don't think you're catching a train either. I think you're here to make money, in which case you need a friend. Wouldn't you like a friend?" He enveloped Maya in his arms and ground his hips against her so that she would know he had something in his pants. Boots's smile faded. The other boys were still, jaws dropped. The security guards leaned forward on their chairs.

Maya tried to duck Yegor's mouth.

The baby had been a brief respite, a period of normality that ended as her witless contribution to the misery of the world.

Who was she to struggle? Whatever shit happened now she deserved.

Zhenya said, "She's with me."

No one had noticed his approach. Yegor let Maya settle on her feet.

"She should've said so. All she had to say was 'I'm with Genius.' What's her name?"

Zhenya told Maya, "Go up to the street."

Yegor asked, "What's the problem? I just asked for her fucking name."

"I'll let you know when she has a name."

"You like her? Does she like you? How much does she like you? Say a hand job is 'like' and anal is 'love.' On that scale where is she? Boots would do anything for me."

"You're a lucky guy."

"You have such a straight face I can never tell when you're agreeing with me and when you're putting a poker up my ass. We're like brothers. The fucking world is falling apart. See how many Tajiks are in Moscow now? Just wait ten years. There'll be a mosque on every corner. Heads cut off, all kinds of stuff. You and I ought to stick together."

"Keep your hands off her."

"Okay. But if you want to be a hero, that will cost you," Yegor shouted as Zhenya started up the stairs. "It will cost you. And a piece of advice. You may have brains but you're not big where it counts. She's going to want a dick. A dick with hair."

Zhenya told Yegor, "Your scarf is wet."

Wet through and through with milk, Yegor discovered.

"What the fuck?"

Attention swung the other way as the Canadian revived and put on a burst of speed toward the far exit. The boys ran after because that was their nature, like puppies chasing a ball, and repeated, "Be-be-be-be-beck in the Yuuessessaarr!"

★

Zhenya led Maya through a courtyard of rubbish bins and cats to a shuttered truck bay and a back door with the bright brass of a new touch pad. He tapped in the combination and, as soon as the door opened, pulled her inside to a freight elevator that carried them up two floors in utter blackness. She clung to his sleeve as he dragged her through a swinging door and the folds of a velvet curtain to a space that, bit by bit, grew into a landscape of drop cloths and cardboard boxes guarded by a giant pulling back his cape to draw his saber.

"Welcome to the Peter the Great Casino," said Zhenya. If he expected thanks he didn't get it. He played the beam of his penlight over the figure's glass eyes and three-corner hat. "It's a good likeness, don't you think?"

She wasn't looking at all. Zhenya couldn't tell whether she was laughing or crying or controlling her rage until in a voice heavy with defeat she asked, "Can you get me a towel? My top is soaked."

He waited outside the ladies' restroom while she washed. Remembering that she had a razor blade, he kept up an aimless chatter through the restroom door.

She wasn't listening. After washing herself and rinsing her shirt, she turned off the lights and sat on a padded stool and rocked. Slowly, as if she were on a moving train.

Immense and unshaven, Willi Pazenko shuffled around the morgue like a woolly mammoth in an operating gown. A cigarette hung from his lips, a glass of antiseptic alcohol from his hand. At school he had been called Belmondo after the French actor for his style with a cigarette. Arkady had been his classmate but now Willi looked twenty years older.

"I can't do it. I'm not up to it. Doctor's orders."

"You could do it with your eyes closed," Arkady said.

Willi waved a glass at the cadavers. "Don't you think I would like to dive in?"

"I know you do."

"Some of the work that comes out of this place you wouldn't believe. Butcher's work at a butcher's pace. A real abattoir. They dig out the heart and lungs, slit the throat and pull out the esophagus. No finesse. No analysis. Run a saw around the skull. Pop the brain. Dig out the organs. Bag them, weigh them, dump them 'tween the knees and finish in less time than it takes to dress a rabbit."

"They must miss things."

"Do they ever! But I'm retired. On the sideline."

Arkady declined a friendly glass of vodka rather than blunt his insomnia. The time was 3 a.m. Insomnia was all he was running on.

Willi said, "I've survived two massive heart attacks. I have angina. Blood pressure that could lift a manhole cover. I could keel over from blowing my nose. So I do not rush."

"What do the doctors say?"

"To lose weight. No smoking or drinking. And avoid excitement. Sex? I haven't seen my dick in years. Some days I can't even find it. Maybe you'd prefer a sparkling wine? I have some cooling in a drawer."

"No, thanks. So you really have moved in? You squared this with the director?"

"The director is a pompous ass but not a bad guy at heart. He found me a spare utility room with a sofa. I'm not supposed to operate anymore because if I expired in the middle of an autopsy, that might lend the impression that the director was not running a tight ship. You not only want me to perform an autopsy, you want it right away." Willi wiped his chin. "My doctors wanted to restrict me to my apartment. Why? To lead the life of a vegetable? Sit alone and watch idiots on television until I expire? No, this is a better solution. Here I still help out with odds and ends. Stay in the social mix. Friends come by, some of them alive, some of them dead, and when I drop, there will be no need for an ambulance because I'll be right here."

"That should be appreciated."

"They tore down my building to make room for a spa. They think they're going to live forever. Are they in for a surprise."

There was a queue of sorts. Other tables held a young male so drained of blood he was white as a marble statue, a barbecued torso of undetermined sex and a bloated body with the last laugh, farts that topped off a general atmosphere of spoiled meat and formaldehyde. Arkady lit a cigarette and drew hard enough that the tobacco sparked and still he tasted bile in his throat.

"Listen to him." Willi indicated the flatulent corpse. "He sounds like he's learning the clarinet."

"What are you now, a music critic?"

"If I was caught performing an autopsy—"

"What could they do to you? They've already got you living in a closet. Are they going to give you a dog bowl next? Whatever happened to Dr. Willi Pazenko? Whatever happened to Belmondo?"

"Belmondo," Willi recollected.

"You don't know how lucky you are." Willi handed Arkady a rubber apron and surgical gloves. "Our assistants are Tajiks or Uzbeks, and when they take the day off for a wedding, everyone else uses it as an excuse to come to work late. Usually this place is humming. Someday the Tajiks are going to take over. They do all that high steel work. Nimble people. But how would you like to fall a hundred stories? All that time to think on the way down."

Arkady declined a surgical mask; masks got clammy and didn't block the smell. Besides, Willi didn't use one. Back in harness, he was thoroughly in command.

"Are you a virgin?" he asked Arkady.

"I've attended."

"But never got your hands dirty, so to speak?"

"No."

"Always a first time."

The external half of the examination of Olga was a search for identifiable features and signs of trauma: birthmarks, moles, scars, needle tracks, bruises, abrasions, tattoos. Willi filled out a chart and body map as he went.

Arkady's job was simple. He lifted Olga as Willi directed. Shifted, posed, positioned her body while Willi snipped an eyelash and a lock of her hair, dug under her fingernails, swabbed and studied every orifice under a UV lamp. Arkady felt like Quasimodo pawing a sleeping Venus.

When the external part of the examination was over, they broke for a cigarette. *Fumo ergo sum*, Arkady thought.

Willi said, "Not a bruise or a scratch. You know that we aren't supposed to open them up unless there are signs of violence or strange circumstances."

"Isn't it strange when a young woman is found half naked and dead?"

"Not when she's a prostitute."

"And the clonidine?"

"This is where your theory falls apart. Clonidine makes a good knockout pill, but it's a messy poison; essentially you throw up and choke on your vomit. I examined her windpipe. It was clean. All you need do is look at her face. She didn't die gasping for air; she just closed her eyes and died."

No one just dies, Arkady thought. You can be killed by a bullet or a skip in your heartbeat or a vine that starts winding around you on the day you are born, but no one just dies.

Willi was warming to the subject. "Any way you look at it, death comes down to oxygen or the lack thereof. Sometimes accomplished with an ax, sometimes with a pillow and almost always leaving evidence. Manual strangulation, for example, is so personal, so over-the-top. Lots of anger and bruising and not only of the neck. I mean, murder is murder, but manual strangulation brings out the worst in people."

"Do you think she removed her panties before or after she died?"

"The panties again?"

"They caught Victor's eye too."

"The last time I saw Detective Orlov he was asleep on a bench on the Boulevard Ring in the middle of the day."

"He's dry tonight."

"So he'll screw up tomorrow and take you down with him, as if you needed any help."

"What do you mean?"

"Tell me, since when does a senior investigator back up a detective sergeant? Does Prosecutor Zurin know what you're up to?"

"It's Victor's case. I'm just along for the ride."

"If Zurin hears about this you've cut your own throat. Well, you can always be my personal assistant."

"Doing what?"

"In case I drop and anyone tries to resuscitate me, shoot him."

Willi started at Olga's left shoulder, drawing the scalpel under the breast and up to the sternum. He shuffled around the table and made a similar cut from the right shoulder. In one masterly stroke, Willi sliced her from the sternum down, opening her all the way to the tattoo.

She looked aside, deaf to the rattle of hardware on the instrument tray: knives and scalpels of different lengths, forceps, UV flashlight and rotary saw. Willi spread open the soft tissue of her chest and selected a garden pruner with curved blades.

"Maybe I should do this," Arkady said.

"When I want an amateur to touch my work, I'll let you know."

Taking that for a no, Arkady reviewed the chart.

Sex: female
Name: unknown

Residence: unknown
Height: 160 cm.
Weight: 49 kg.
Hair: brown
Eyes: blue
Estimated Time of Death: by core temperature and
start of rigor approximately 2 to 3 hours previous

Her ribs snapped with the sound of green wood cracking. Arkady read on.

Observations: The deceased was delivered at 0216 dressed in a blue jacket of synthetic material and a white cotton bustier. Two plastic bags arrived with the body. Bag A contained items found on site: a blue denim skirt with decorative stitching and knee-high red boots of faux leather. Underpants were retrieved from an upper bunk in the trailer. Bag B held personal effects that included cosmetics, pepper spray, diaphragm, douche and an aspirin bottle that contained a yellow powder that preliminary toxicological examination has tentatively identified as clonidine, a blood pressure medication sometimes abused as a "knockout" pill.

UV radiation was used to examine the body, jacket and bustier for fingerprints, semen or blood. The result was negative. No bruising, stains or signs of forcible sexual entry. No signs of strangulation either manual or ligature. Bands of pale skin indicated the recent removal of rings from the 3rd, 4th and 5th fingers of the left hand and the 3rd and 4th fingers of the right. The deceased exhibited superficial dirt on her hands and face.

Body in excellent physical condition. Distinguishing marks: tattoo on cusp of left hip. No scars or birthmarks or occupational calluses. No evident lacerations or contusions. No signs of struggle or defensive wounds. No hypodermic needle tracks. No body piercing except earlobes. Material under fingernails was unremarkable.

Willi paused to ask Arkady, "You okay?"

"I'm fine."

Arkady was eight years old on his first visit to a morgue. His father took him to toughen him up. Arkady remembered the general slapping a dead man on the ass and declaring, "He served under me in Kursk!" Some men could saunter into a morgue and browse autopsy tables like a garden show. Arkady had never attained such sangfroid. After twenty years as an investigator he was still as embarrassed by an eviscerated body as if he had caught someone undressed.

With the ribs out of the way Willi detached the girl's heart and lungs and put them together, en bloc, into a pail held by Arkady. In other pails went other organs, wet and glistening as strange sea creatures.

Next, up or down? Up it was.

Olga's hair was thick and vigorous, but with a hairbrush and comb Willi created a part from ear to ear, retraced the part with a scalpel and peeled the top half of the face down to the chin from a red skull and startled eyes.

While Willi sawed, Arkady's mind wandered. He thought about vodka, about Victor's limitless thirst and the half-empty bottle found with Olga. A dirty mattress in a workers' wagon didn't seem appealing even for a prostitute. Yet they hadn't run in and out. Olga and her friend had opened a bottle and stayed long enough for one to dope the other. A toast! How do you toast without glasses? Arkady thought about the tattoo's deep colors and distinct lines, the work of a professional, not a prison camp lifer working with an unsterilized needle and paid for in cigarettes. What species was Olga's butterfly? The writer Nabokov had always been enchanted by "blues," a category of butterflies that were small and drab until they flew and then their wings were iridescent.

Willi repaired the damage. He sewed the body together with twine and the scalp together with black sutures although the girl was largely a hollow, her organs set aside in buckets and bowls and her brain deposited in a jar of formalin to harden enough to slice, which would take at least a week. Quite a night for Olga, Arkady thought. First she is killed and then she is rearranged. Maybe cannibals lurked around the corner.

Soaked with perspiration, Willi dropped onto a stool next to the table, two fingers monitoring the pulse in his neck, giving Arkady a few seconds to worry about Zhenya. Was he running with a street gang? Arrested for hustling? Beaten to death by a sore loser? With Zhenya, anxiety was on tap twenty-four hours a day.

Willi shook his head. "Steady as a Swiss watch."

"Do you really want to die in the middle of an autopsy? Why don't you just run around the block?"

"I hate exercise."

Willi poured more alcohol and this time Arkady joined him. It went down smoothly and then set his throat on fire.

"Needs lemon."

Voices came from the hall of body drawers and Willi straightened up. When the sound subsided he asked Arkady, "Is there anything you want to add to the chart? Anything I missed?"

Since pathologists were used to having the final say, Arkady chose his words carefully.

"You mention the dirt under her fingernails but you don't mention that her nails are manicured. Same with her toenails."

"Women paint their nails. Since when is that worth mentioning?"

"Her clothes."

"She dressed like a slut."

"Her outfit was shabby but it was new. The boots were poor quality but they were also new."

"You're thinking far too much about this girl."

"Then there's the lack of bruises and scratches, the wear and tear that a person accumulates from having sex with nasty customers in alleyways and trailers."

Willi blew a smoke ring in Arkady's direction. "Old friend, take it from a man with one foot in the grave, everything is contradictory. Stalin was good then bad then good again. Once I was thin as a reed and now I'm a human globe with a belt as my equator. In any case, don't be distressed over a dead prostitute. There's a new one every day. If she isn't claimed she will make some medical student very happy, and if someone claims her, I'll let you know. This was my last autopsy."

"Too bad it was a failure," Arkady said.

Willi reacted as if slapped. "What do you mean by that?"

"An autopsy is supposed to determine the cause of death. You failed."

"Arkady, I found what was there. I can't manufacture evidence."

"You missed it."

They were interrupted by the arrival of the morgue director and a woman in a black shawl. The director was surprised by the sight of Willi and Arkady but regained enough poise to lead her around the autopsy tables with the smoothness of a maître d'. She strode. She was one of those women who seemed to have been bronzed at her peak, forty going on thirty, in dark glasses and shadowy silk. She gave Willi and Arkady no more than a glance.

The director led her to the table of the suicide and after a sympathetic cough asked if she could identify the body.

The woman said, "This is Sergei Petrovich Borodin. My son."

Even drained of color, Sergei Borodin was handsome, with longish hair that still seemed damp from the bath. He was about twenty years old, lean through the chest and muscular from the waist down. His mother's emotion was hidden by her dark glasses but Arkady assumed grief was involved. She took her dead boy's hand and turned his wrist to a decisive slash.

Meanwhile the director explained the cost of generating a death certificate for a bathroom fall. The paramedics who found the body would have to change their reports. They would expect to be rewarded. In the meantime the morgue was willing to store the body for a fee.

"To rent a drawer?"

"A refrigerated drawer that size . . ."

"Of course. Go on."

"In these circumstances I would suggest a generous donation to the church for a service in his name and a Christian burial."

"Is that it?"

"And your son's certificate of residence."

"He had no certificate of residence. He was a dancer. He stayed with friends and other artists."

"Even artists must obey the law. I'm sorry, there will be a fine."

She turned her son's wrist to the director. "I won't make a fuss if you sew this."

He was eager to redeem himself. "It's no problem. Is there anything else we can do?"

"Burn him."

The director paused. "Cremate him? We don't do that here."

"Then arrange it."

Like a thunderclap, Willi sneezed. The woman's attention snapped to him and then to Arkady. She removed her dark glasses to see better and her dry eyes were more naked than anything else in the room. Then at full speed she was gone, the director at her heels.

"I'm sorry," Arkady said. "I'm afraid I put you in a bad spot."

"The hell with it. I hate sleeping on a sofa." Willi was in surprisingly high spirits.

"And, besides your heart problems, now you have a cold?"

"No. Something tickled my nose. Something penetrated this atmosphere of putrefaction and formaldehyde. A trained nose is important. Every schoolboy should recognize the smell of garlic for arsenic and almonds for cyanide. Hand me the lungs. Let's discover what your lady friend last breathed."

Arkady transferred from pail to tray the girl's heart and lungs still attached, a fist of muscle between two spongy loaves. He smelled nothing that penetrated the usual miasma until Willi sliced the left lung and released a sweet whiff.

"Ether."

"Ether exactly," Willi agreed. "It's taking a while to dissipate because she didn't breathe again. So it was in two stages: clonidine to knock her out and ether to anesthetize and kill her, all without a struggle. Congratulations, you have a murder."

Arkady's cell phone chimed twice only, and by the time he freed himself from the autopsy apron and dug the phone out of a pocket, he had missed a call from Zhenya, the first communication from the boy in a week. Arkady immediately returned the call but Zhenya didn't answer, which struck Arkady as a fair example of their relationship.

Or that whatever Zhenya had called about was fleeting and unimportant.

7

Maya sat at the vanity in a Peter the Great restroom with a towel over her shoulders while Zhenya shaved her head. She had cut off her red hair with office scissors but there were places she couldn't see or reach with a razor, and although she resented the forced intimacy of the situation, she bowed her head while Zhenya scraped away with a razor from the dealers' lounge. Cutting her hair was his idea; her red hair as good as pointed her out to the militia. Now she was as bald as a chick.

"Did you ever shave anyone's head before?"

"No."

"Have you ever shaved yourself?"

"No."

"That's what I thought."

They had barely slept because she wanted to meet the six-thirty train at Yaroslavl Station, the same train that she had been on, hopefully with the same crew. Auntie Lena had claimed she was such a regular passenger that people knew her up and down the line. Maybe someone did.

The mirror doubled her misery. She imagined the kind of women usually reflected in such looking glasses as tall and sophisticated, drinking champagne as they gambled, laughing lightly whether they won or lost. Why not? They had better odds at roulette than she had of finding her baby.

She asked, "Why isn't anyone here?"

"The Peter the Great Casino has been closed for weeks. A lot of casinos are closed."

"Why?"

"Arkady says Moscow wants to project a dignified image like other world capitals. He says someone in the Kremlin noticed that there aren't any slot machines on the steps of the White House or Buckingham Palace."

She wondered why anyone would steal a baby. What did they do with babies? How could she have gone to sleep and let her baby be stolen? She didn't ask for these questions, they came unbidden ten times a second. Which reminded her how her breasts ached; she would have to milk herself like a cow before she left for the station. She had made up her mind that Zhenya was staying behind. He meant well but it was like having a squirrel on her shoulder, and, although it was irrational to blame Zhenya, the sight of her hair falling into a wastebasket was as depressing as losing her name.

She asked, "You and Yegor are friends?"

"We have a business arrangement."

"What does that mean?"

"I play chess for money. It's a business that's easily disrupted. I pay Yegor for protection."

"From who?"

"From Yegor, basically."

"You punk out to him? You don't defend yourself?"

"It's a business expense. It's hard to play chess when four guys jump you and another kicks the board. If more people learned how to play without a board, there wouldn't be a problem. I could teach you."

"To punk out? No, thanks. Maybe I should ask Yegor for help."

"I wouldn't advise it."

"Why?"

"He thinks you're attractive."

"Are you jealous?"

Zhenya concentrated solemnly on the crown of her skull. Her scalp was coming up a faint blue and as smooth as a billiard ball.

"Just avoid him."

"Have you ever had a girlfriend?"

He didn't have any answer to that. He might be a genius but he was also a virgin. She could tell by how timidly he blew cuttings from the nape of her neck.

"So Yegor is the guy in charge."

"He thinks he's in charge."

"Why didn't you ask him about my baby?"

"The less you see of Yegor the better."

"You could have asked."

Yegor's name was a drop of ink in water. Everything took a darker shade.

She asked, "So how come you have the run of this place?"

"I know the combination for the keypad."

"You are such a liar. Anyway, nobody plays chess for money."

"How would you know what people do in Moscow?"

That let her know that she was a peasant. They finished the rest of the shave in silence until Zhenya toweled her off.

"Do you want to take a look in the mirror?"

"No. Is there a refrigerator here?"

"An ice bin at the bar. We've got everything. Nuts, pretzels, chips—"

"Can you get me a glass and napkins and then leave me alone?"

From the vantage point of the casino Zhenya watched Maya push through the early-morning crowds of Three Stations. The rain made cars appear to crawl over one another. Yesterday Maya had been a flamboyant rebel in red. Today she was a gray figure with a knit cap pulled over a shaved head, as common as a crow. Without a backward glance she went down the steps of the underpass and disappeared.

He did consider calling Arkady but to tell him what? That a mental case searching for an imaginary baby didn't want his help? She had come and gone like a bad dream, taking his knife with her. The only other evidence of her visit was a nest of dyed hair in a wastebasket and in the bar fridge a quarter glass of mother's milk. He shouldn't have taken Maya in. What was he thinking? Not even Arkady knew about this hideaway. No one knew that it was his.

Before the crackdown the casino had buzzed with color. Outside, a neon Peter the Great had opened and closed the lid of a neon chest heaped with crown jewels. Inside, players were welcomed by the lifelike wax figure of Peter, all seven feet of him in a mantle of golden threads trimmed in fur, indicating with an outstretched arm the way to the high-stakes tables, although from certain angles there was something familiar in the twist of his mouth that inspired the nickname Putin the Great.

At that time Zhenya's only connection to the Peter the Great was a guard named Yakov who styled himself a serious chess player even though he knew no more than basic openings, like the diagrammed floor of a dance class. When he opened his jacket to be comfortable, a shoulder holster couldn't help but peek out. Every Wednesday evening they played at the buffet in Yaroslavl Station, Yakov agonizing over every move because there seemed to be no plan of attack simple enough for him to remember. Zhenya toyed with him, letting him almost win, but it was impossible to lose to a man who consistently brought out his queen too soon and castled too late.

The last time they met, Zhenya noticed numbers written in ballpoint on the palm of Yakov's hand and asked if they were moves. At once Yakov went in the direction of the restroom to wash his hands. Zhenya paused the game clock and waited.

After half an hour he realized that the guard was not coming back. Zhenya paid for a sandwich he had not eaten, stuffed his chess paraphernalia into his daypack and ventured out to the square. Evening made the shabby stalls, kiosks and video game galleries busy and bright. All but Peter the Great. A neon replica of Czar Peter, Emperor of all the Russias, was unplugged, a black hole amid the glitter. Two uniformed militia officers stood at the casino's front entrance.

No one knew the shortcuts and courtyards of Three Stations better than the runaways that Zhenya moved among. He slipped into the shadow of the neighboring courtyard, climbed a pyramid of tires to the top of the wall and lowered himself to the lid of a rubbish bin in the courtyard of the casino. The truck bay was shut from the back door and was guarded by a keyless lock with an illuminated numerical pad. Of course, when the casino was up and running, there would have been armed guards and security cameras.

The plate of the lock was brass, unscratched, absolutely new, necessitating a new combination that Yakov apparently had trouble remembering. All the same, was there a parallel system? A silent alarm or a wailing siren? Braced to run, Zhenya punched in the numbers he had glimpsed on Yakov's hand and the door opened with a sigh.

Thus Zhenya claimed the Peter the Great Casino. Nothing unusual about it. So many runaways squatted in the railway cars, basements, empty buildings and construction sites of Moscow that the mayor called them "rats." And although Zhenya was a trespasser, he felt at home. More so than in the rusting Khrushchev-era flats he had shared with his father or in any children's shelter or being under Arkady's eye.

Even if he had to live in it as quietly as a ghost, the casino was the first private place Zhenya had ever lived. And if they caught him, what could the consequences be? He hadn't vandalized the place; if anything, he took care of it.

Glossy brochures described the Peter the Great as *only one star in a galaxy of entertainment venues offered by VGI, the Vaksberg Group International*. Apparently VGI owned twenty other casinos in Moscow, some much grander than the Peter the Great, not to mention gaming establishments in London, Barbados and Dubai. A company like VGI had friends as well as enemies in the Kremlin. The standoff could go on for quite a while.

So the boy lived at Three Stations in a bubble, alone, above the crowd. Every day he explored the count room, the cashier's cage, the corridor behind one-way mirrors, the security room with its elastic restraints. Black jackets and bow ties hung in the dealers' lounge. Zhenya wore a tie loose around his neck and imagined the envy of VIPs and the awe of beautiful women as he approached the roulette table with the long, confident strides of a new Bobby Fischer.

The rain continued. Zhenya spent half the day by the casino window before he saw Maya standing on the curb in front of Leningrad Station. Something wayward about her made him think that she didn't know or care where she was. She pushed the hood of her jacket back and lifted her face to the sky, her scalp a naked blue.

She wasn't Zhenya's problem. It only irritated him that he

had confided in her enough to reveal his access to Peter the Great and break his own rules about not entering or leaving the casino in the daytime, no lights at night and, most of all, no visitors. The casino was his realm as long as he was alone.

The militia no longer posted men at the casino. Police cars cruised by from time to time and tugged on the padlock on the front entrance but they never bothered with the courtyard in back. Zhenya concluded that the militia had been kept ignorant of the combination to prevent everything that wasn't bolted down from disappearing in the middle of the night.

In the meantime the ventilation system automatically cleaned the air. Champagne was chilled and the icemaker filled to the brim. The owners could walk in and have their casino up and running within an hour.

For Zhenya the casino was a theme park. In the daytime he could lie down on the carpet and take in sparkling chandeliers and murals of virgins preparing for a visit from Peter, who claimed a monarch's right to sample the beauties of his empire, from hot-eyed Circassian exotics to buxom, blue-eyed girls of the Ukraine. The painter had captured each in a state of high anticipation.

At night the carpet was softer than some beds he had known. The slot machines were musketeers in caftans with recorded encouragement like, "One more for the czar!" Zhenya lifted the cloth off the roulette table and found everything in place: blue baize, plaques, winning markers, croupier rakes.

He spun the wheel and tossed a silvery ball counter to the blur of red and black numbers. While the ball rode the rim the sound was circular, and as the ball lost momentum it clicked off diamond-shaped studs, hopped erratically from one slot to another and finally came to rest on "0," the house's number.

He picked up the ball again and threw it the length of the gaming room. Swept a stack of candy-red $50,000 plaques to the floor. Kicked a box that exploded into poker chips.

Arkady expected that when he returned to Yaroslavl Station he would find the trailer lit like a circus tent. Instead, his headlights found only Victor with a bloody nose.

"The trailer's gone." Victor pressed a handkerchief against his nose. "It was Colonel Malenkov and his men. They towed it away. Malenkov said it was a public nuisance."

"Did Malenkov know he was towing away a crime scene?"

"The colonel says there was no crime. That you can sit on your dick and spin, because he is still carrying our Olga on the books as an overdose. He likes his statistics the way they are. How does the nose look?"

"Crusting up nicely. What happened?"

"Some pushing and shoving."

"The colonel can't make all the evidence disappear. Willi found clonidine in her stomach and a lethal dose of ether in her lungs. What's the matter?"

"I don't see a lot of official backup around here. I just see you and me out on a limb."

"This is a good case, Victor."

"Then why are we alone?"

"It's an advantage."

"An advantage? Do you appreciate the futility of one man talking to a hundred prostitutes and crazies to find a single sober, reliable witness? If I'd asked, 'Has anyone seen a giant lizard?' I might've gotten somewhere. We have no identification, no witness, no scene of the crime and no support.' Victor looked wistfully toward a kiosk with shelves of vodka. Arkady felt the plunge in Victor's mood and could feel the power of his thirst.

"Have you got a good suit?" Arkady asked.

"What?"

"Do you have something appropriate to wear to the Nijinsky Fair tonight? We have an invitation but we have to blend in."

"You and me with millionaires?"

"I'm afraid so. They've had some bad times lately."

"Huh. What should I say to a bloodsucker who's lost a million dollars?"

"You express compassion."

"I could kill him and feed him to the pigs."

"Well, something in between."

Apartment lights came on in the high-rise across from the station. Wives would be dressing themselves, pulling clothes on children, making breakfast. Men would be sitting on the edge of the bed, smoking the first cigarette of the day and wondering what had happened to their lives.

Eva, for example, had disappeared from Arkady's life like an actress who, in the middle of a play, decided that if her lines in Act I were poor, her lines in Act II were no better. She sent Arkady a note that said, *I will not wait around until they kill you.*

I won't be the grieving widow of a man who insists on teasing the executioners of the state. I will not be there when someone shoots you in your car or answering the doorbell and I won't walk in your funeral cortege.

Arkady thought that was a little harsh. Backward even, considering she was a medical volunteer who answered the siren call of every disaster. That they had met at Chernobyl was a bad sign. They loved each other, only the half-life of that love was shorter than he had supposed.

Victor said, "We're back where we started with Olga. I checked with Missing Persons. Nobody's missed her yet."

"We can cover the apartments together."

"Do we have to? I mean, what's the point? No one cares about a dead prostitute."

"What if she's not?" Arkady asked. "What if Olga was not a prostitute?"

"You're joking."

"What if she's not?"

"Excuse me, but the only thing we know for certain about this case is that Olga was a prostitute. She dressed like a prostitute, was tattooed like a prostitute and she pulled off her panties like a prostitute in a trailer no normal person would set foot in."

"What everybody notices about her is that she doesn't have a scratch or a bruise. No needle tracks. Victor, show me a prostitute here that isn't damaged one way or the other."

"She was new in the game is all. See, I know what you're up to. You're trying to keep me too busy to drink. I'm not a dog you keep busy chasing a ball." Victor had a vicious grin. "I'd kill for a drink."

"Where are her rings? From her tan lines she had five rings on her fingers. They weren't in her bag."

"Probably the man she was with took them. Maybe that's what was going on, a robbery."

"For a streetwalker's jewelry? Did you get any pictures?"
Victor produced a pocket-size video camera.
"Enjoy."

The first image on the view panel was Olga as she was found half naked on the mattress, her head turned, her legs crossed so that her right heel touched her left toe. Her right arm was raised overhead as if she were a bride tossing her bouquet over her shoulder. Victor had carried out some interviews. The prostitutes were righteously pleased that an interloper had been eliminated. Pimps turned away. Street boys were disappointed that the body was not on display. The homeless asked for loose change. Drunks screwed up their faces in confusion. All in all, they constituted a human menagerie, not a witness pool.

Arkady rewound back to Olga.

"That's an unnatural position."

"So?"

"As if he killed her and arranged her body. He pulled her panties off so that we would gape. Gape and not see." Arkady thought there was just a chance that someone in the dark glowed with pride. He looked up at the apartment building on the other side of the station, at balconies with a perfect view.

The building was eight stories high, six one-bedroom apartments to a floor. Victor and Arkady called only on the five apartments that had been lit when they first answered the radio call.

Apartment 2C. Volchek and Primakov, bear-size Siberians with furtive eyes. Both loggers, thirty-five years of age, in rooms so cold the air conditioner shivered. The scent of something rotten was coated by the floral spray of an air freshener. A saw lay in the bathtub. In the refrigerator, mold and a case of beer. They said they had played cards and watched DVDs all night. Arkady pictured them swatting salmon in a stream.

Apartment 4F. Weitzman, ninety, widower, retired metallurgist, observant Jew who took seriously the Torah's injunction against operating equipment during Shabbos. From sunset Friday to sunset Saturday even flicking an electrical switch or turning a dial was forbidden. If he wanted to take the elevator, he had to ride it until someone went to his floor. He had shaped his life to take into account every possible misstep, but he had nodded off during a television documentary on Putin's early years—*Just Another Boy!*—and awoke to a rebroadcast of the same show. He had seen the documentary six times so far. When Arkady turned off the set it was like cutting a man down from the rack.

Apartment 4D. Army General Kassel, forty-two, answered the door in a civilian raincoat and shoes.

The general was a resident of Petersburg in Moscow on what he claimed was military business, although Arkady saw expended champagne bottles on the floor and heard a woman sobbing in the bedroom.

In a whisper Kassel said he was only passing through and hadn't noticed a black trailer in the dark at a hundred meters and knew nothing about any activity there.

Arkady asked the general how long he had been awake.

"You woke me up."

Victor asked, "Were you here all night?"

"With my wife."

"Who besides your wife?"

"No one."

A bad lie poorly told unless Kassel slept half dressed. And the array of dirty glasses and full ashtrays were the remains of a larger party than two. Also Kassel's weight was forward on the balls of his feet, waiting for something, anticipating something.

But if Kassel was hiding something, who wasn't? As Victor liked to say, "That's the problem with interrogations, so many lies, so little time."

Apartment 3C. Anna Furtseva at eighty-eight was a living legend. Arkady and Victor didn't know she was that Anna Furtseva until the door was opened by a small, imperious woman in a rich caftan, lips mainly lipstick and eyes outlined in kohl. Behind her stood life-size photographs of black men with penis sheaths and hair adorned with feathers of birds of paradise. Of Masai warriors mixing a drink of milk and blood. Of Russian convicts covered in tattoos.

"You'll have some tea," Furtseva said. It was a statement, not a question.

While she bustled to the kitchen Arkady took in the rest of the apartment, a magpie's nest of the exotic and almost junk: a Persian carpet, ottomans with split leather, Mexican serapes, Balinese puppets, stuffed monkeys and photographs on every surface. Across the room an ancient wolfhound sighed.

Victor saluted photographs of a young Furtseva with Hemingway, Kennedy, Yevtushenko and Fidel.

"The major cocksmen of our time."

"Pardon?" Furtseva returned with a tray of tea, sugar and jam.

"Your photographs are a major comment on our time," Arkady said.

"Ahead of its time," Victor maintained.

Furtseva poured. "Yes. We called the show of the three men *Evolution*. It was 1972. The KGB tore it down the same day we put it up. We resisted but we were goldfish against sharks. I am surprised you even heard of it."

"But it was historic," Victor said.

"With history goes age. Age is overrated. Do notice the portraits of dancers on the piano. From Nijinsky to Baryshnikov." They were all male and captured in midair, except for an older man in a white suit hanging back in the shadow of a doorway. "I'm afraid Nijinsky was a little gaga by the time I caught up with him."

He and Victor sank into ottomans while Furtseva settled in a chair, her legs tucked up in a girlish fashion. It struck

Arkady that if Cleopatra had lived to eighty-eight she would
have looked a little like Furtseva. Everything was done with a
flourish. When the wolfhound farted, Furtseva lit a match and
burned off the methane in the air with a royal wave. "Now tell
me what this is all about. I'm on pins and needles. I saw an
ambulance take someone from the trailer. Did somebody die?"

"A girl," Victor said. "Probably from an overdose, but we
have to consider every possibility. Were you awake at midnight?"

"Of course."

"Do you suffer from insomnia?"

"I benefit from insomnia. However, I have developed a problem with sunlight. I can't let any into the apartment. I have to
draw these ridiculous blue shades during the day and I can only
go out at night. The joke is on me since I'm a photographer."

Victor said, "So you do still take photographs."

"Oh, yes. Such interesting characters to see at Three Stations. Like creatures at a watering hole."

Victor politely dunked his sugar cube. "Did you see the
trailer being taken away?"

"Of course."

"Did you notice anyone go in or out of the trailer before it
was taken away?"

"No. Was the girl a prostitute?"

"That's all we know for sure."

"I suppose the trailer was taken away for more analysis?"

Near the Arctic Circle, Arkady thought.

The dog hiccuped and Furtseva opened a fresh box of
matches.

Victor asked, "You saw nothing unusual tonight?"

"Apart from the removal of the trailer, no. I'm sorry, gentlemen."

Victor stood and almost bowed. "Thank you, Madame
Furtseva, for the excellent tea. If you remember something else,

anything at all, please call me. I'm leaving you my card." He laid it by his cup.

She hesitated. "There is one thing. I suppose it's totally unrelated."

"Please. You never know."

"Well, my downstairs neighbors, the two Siberians . . ."

"Volchek and Primakov. We've met them."

"Not tonight but the night before, they snuck into the building with body bags. Full bags. Yesterday I got off on the wrong floor—they all look the same, you know—and before I put my key in the door, I heard them talk about dismembering a body."

Furtseva's eyes shined.

Arkady joined the conversation. "You were snooping."

"Not intentionally."

"Did you try your key in the lock?"

"No."

"How long were you at the door?"

"A few seconds. Ten at the most."

"Did they open the door?"

"Yes, but I sent the elevator to the top while I took the stairs holding my shoes."

"A close call."

"Yes."

"You're very pleased with yourself."

"You don't have to whisper. My hearing is excellent."

"Do you wear eyeglasses?"

"For reading."

"For reading but not for distance? Do you understand what I mean by distance?"

"I was a filmmaker in the war. I learned how to calculate distance at Stalingrad."

This was dangerous, Arkady thought. He and Victor were walking on their knees from lack of sleep. Thanks for the tea, but the last thing they needed was a legend aching for adventure. From the alarm on Victor's face he finally grasped the peril they were in.

Arkady said, "Very well, Madame Furtseva, please tell me carefully what Volchek and Primakov said. Their exact words."

"Exactly?"

"Exactly."

"In that Siberian drawl of theirs one said, 'Where do I bury her fucking head?' The other said, 'Up your ass, where your head is.' The first one said, 'She's going to leave a real mess in the fucking van.' The second one said, 'Stop shitting your pants. She's been dead long enough; she's not going to bleed.' Then they suddenly stopped talking and that's when I left the door."

She lit a match as if for punctuation.

Arkady said, "These are not men to fool around with. Have you seen them since then?"

"No, but I certainly heard them."

"Tonight?"

"Yes."

"Could you put a time to that?"

"Since dinner. I heard them swearing and drinking beer and watching football."

Victor asked, "You're absolutely sure, Madame Furtseva? All night? Here?"

"Every minute."

"Did they seem to show any interest when the trailer was removed?"

"No."

"Did they ever show any interest in the trailer anytime?"

"No."

Victor spread his arms in relief. The Siberians could slaughter victims left and right, but as long as they had no connection to the trailer, this was somebody else's mess.

Watching Maya was agony. Zhenya watched her futile attempts to accost passengers as they stepped off the morning train from Yaroslavl. Now the isolation she had maintained during the trip worked against her. No one remembered her red hair or her baby. No one had ever heard of Auntie Lena. She mentioned the card game and arguments. Like every other ride in hard class, people said. They were going to work. No time to talk. She ran after a priest she remembered by the crumbs on his beard. This time he wore a faint dusting of confectioners' sugar. He had no recollection of her.

Zhenya saw Maya wilt under the maddening interrogation of babushkas. Darling, how could you lose a baby? Did you pray to Saint Christopher, dear? Was it your little brother? This never would have happened in the old days. Are you on drugs? At least when a Gypsy begs you see the baby.

Including platforms, cafés, waiting rooms, tunnels, anterooms, nursery, ticket booths, there was too much ground to cover. Pedestrian underpasses were bottlenecked by shops and salesladies who wasted her time with scissors and clippers and hose until Maya wanted to scream. Finally she found herself in the main hall of the train station like a chess piece with every move exhausted.

Not every move, Zhenya reminded himself. There was her razor and a wide selection of trains. In a mosaic of families and traders rising with the sun she was in free fall.

Zhenya took a chair next to Maya. She didn't acknowledge him but she didn't leave. They sat like travelers, staring heavy-lidded at the digital clock above the arrival and departure board. As fatigue won out over fury her breathing slowed and her body relaxed. He figured that she hadn't eaten since the day before and handed her a candy bar.

"Did that woman call?"

It took him a moment to guess what woman she meant.

"The platform woman? No, she hasn't called yet. She has my cell-phone number."

"You're sure?"

"I put it in her hand."

"She seemed a good person."

Zhenya shrugged. Social skills were not his strong point. In fact, for Zhenya, one of the most appealing aspects of chess was that victory was self-evident. Screw conversation. The winning player need not say anything other than "check" and "mate." The problem was that Zhenya was always either boastful or mute. Sometimes when he heard himself he wondered, Who is this jackass? He was aware how miserably he had failed in his first go-round with Maya. The moment was getting strained but he had to say something because militia with rubber truncheons had entered the waiting room to roust any homeless who had snuck in. The officers were led by the lieutenant who had chased Maya.

Zhenya said, "Let's get some air."

"We'll come back?"

"Yes."

"Without the investigator?"

Her head shaved, her eyes seemed huge.

"You two!"

The lieutenant saw them when they stood. His attention was diverted, however, by a street boy who snatched a purse and bolted for the underpass. Zhenya steered Maya away from the chase and out the station's double doors to what he had always regarded as an open-air market of crap. Crap toys, crap souvenirs, crap fur hats, crap posters under a crap sky of floating shit. Today, he embraced it.

They browsed the stalls. To extend Maya's wardrobe Zhenya bought her T-shirts featuring the Stones, Putin and Kurt Cobain; a knockoff sweatshirt from Cafe Hollywood; a cap from Saint-Tropez and a wig of human hair from India. Maya went along in a bemused way, as if she had caught him playing with dolls, until they reached a kiosk that sold cell phones. Zhenya decided that she should have a mobile phone in case they became separated.

The kiosk was so crammed with electronic and video gear that the two vendors inside had to move in tandem. They were Albanians, father and son, practically clones, in tight shirts unbuttoned to display gold chains and body hair. They were willing to sell Zhenya a top-quality cell phone and SIM card, no contract and no monthly charges. No rip-offs. They showed Zhenya an unbroken seal on the box of a similar phone.

"It's stolen," Zhenya said.

The vendors laughed and looked at each other.

"What are you talking about?"

"The bar code. It's simple. Drop the first and last bars, break the rest into groups of five, add the digits under the long bars and you have your zip code. You can get the delivery point too. This box was supposed to go from Hanover, Germany, to Warsaw, Poland. It was hijacked on the way. You should show this to the militia. Would you like me to check your other boxes?"

People stopped to listen to Zhenya's flat robotic voice.

"The other boxes?"

"All the boxes."

More people gathered. Traditionally no market was complete without entertainment, a puppet show or a dancing bear. Zhenya was today's.

He said, "I shouldn't have to pay full price for something stolen. And the warranty is probably no good when the goods are stolen."

The son said, "Get out of here, you fucking freak."

The old man, however, was aware that a sizable crowd was developing. He was protected against acts of violence such as arson or a brick through a window, not agitation from a wiseass who could read a bar code. Besides, strangling the creep right now might drag in the militia, which was like inviting in locusts.

"Let me take care of the little prick." The younger vendor started out of the kiosk only to be held back by his father, who told Zhenya, "Pay no attention. So, my young sir, what do you think would be a fair price?"

"Half off."

"I'll throw in some phone cards, too, as a proof of no ill will."

"In a bag."

"As you wish." The father turned on a smile. A murmur of approval ran through the crowd.

As soon as Zhenya and Maya were gone, another shopper stepped up to the kiosk and asked the father for the same discount.

The old man turned on him. "Can you read a bar code?"

"No."

"Then go fuck yourself."

Zhenya had never noticed before how interesting the market was with all its pirated CDs of hip-hop and heavy metal, T-shirts of Che and Michael Jackson, Chinese parasols, Muscovites with their noses in the air, women from Central Asia dragging a suitcase the size of an elephant calf, the sound of explosions rocking a game arcade while drunks reposed against a wall. That was pulsating life, wasn't it? More so than any plaster animal decoration on the station wall.

"Was that a trick back there with the bar code?" Maya asked. "How did you do that?"

"A magician never reveals his secrets."

"What other secrets do you have?"

"They'd be pretty poor secrets if I told you."

"Is that why they call you 'genius,' because of the tricks and the chess?"

"The trick of the bar code is that there is no trick. You just do the math."

"Oh."

"And as for chess, it's basically a matter of anticipating your opponent's moves. You go step-by-step. The more you play the easier it gets to cover every possibility."

"Do you ever lose?"

"Sure. You have to let your opponent win at the start to raise the stakes. It's not about winning the game; it's about taking their money. That's the game inside the game." He ducked under a display of condoms that promised long-lasting pleasure in a variety of colors and certainly were an improvement over the old Soviet galosh. The words popped into his mouth. "Who is the baby's father?"

"It could be anybody."

It was the one answer that Zhenya had not anticipated.

10

★

This wasn't Arkady's Moscow anymore. The Golden Mile—the area between the Kremlin and the Church of the Redeemer—had been a neighborhood of workers, students and artists. The local restaurants were stand-up cafeterias that served steamed cabbage. The streets glittered not with diamonds but broken glass. But that population was gone. Bought out, sold out, "developed" out, they had been relocated and replaced by boutiques and leggy women with Prada bags who circulated from Pilates class to tapas bar, from tapas bar to sushi, from raw fish to meditation.

Since the Lada's muffler sounded like a snare drum, Arkady pulled to the curb to call Zhenya. Sometimes the boy withdrew for weeks and what Arkady feared was his isolation. Besides the chess players he hustled, Zhenya had no regular human contact that Arkady knew of except for a gang of runaways led by a dangerous young thug named Yegor who was suspected of setting homeless people on fire.

Ten rings without an answer was Arkady's limit. He no sooner gave up than a white SUV loomed alongside and a woman with sunglasses perched on her forehead motioned for him to roll down his window. A silk scarf was knotted casually around her neck and a gold chain dangled from her wrist.

She said, "This is a 'No Lada Zone.'"

"A what zone?"

"Ladas."

"Like this car?"

"Correct. No Ladas are allowed to park in the zone, let alone to sleep in."

Arkady looked at Victor snoring in a rubbery fashion.

"We are in Russia?" Arkady asked.

"Yes."

"In Moscow?"

"Yes, of course."

"And the Lada is a Russian car?"

"One Lada can reduce the value of an entire city block."

"I had no idea."

"I mean, were you towed here?"

"Passing through."

"I knew it. 'Through traffic' is the worst. Why did you stop?"

"We're releasing rats."

"That's it. I'm alerting Security."

Arkady's cell phone rang. Because he expected a callback from Zhenya, he answered without checking the caller.

"Thank you," Zurin said. "You actually picked up for once. This will be like a birthday present but better."

Arkady rolled up his window. When the woman started another diatribe, he held up his ID. A moment later the SUV melted and she was gone.

"What would be better?"

"Your letter of resignation."

"I haven't given you one."

"No hurry, Renko, you have all day."

For Arkady, Prosecutor Zurin exemplified the modest ambition of a cork. It floated. In regime after regime, policy after counterpolicy, Zurin floated and survived.

"Why would I resign?"

"Because the last thing you want is a departmental hearing for suspension."

"Why should I be suspended?"

"You disregard orders and overstep your authority and regularly hold the office of the prosecutor up to ridicule."

"Could you be more specific?"

"The business with a dead unidentified prostitute. You were told not to initiate any investigations."

"I didn't. I was with a militia officer who responded to the radio call of an overdose after the local precinct failed to answer. I assisted the officer when, with the exception of forensic technicians, no support arrived."

"What support do you need for an OD? You gave me your head on a silver platter. All you had to do was stay in the car."

"It's not an OD," Arkady said. "According to the pathologist, the girl was administered—"

"You miss the point. You ignored my orders. You were not authorized to order an autopsy."

"Detective Orlov is and it's his case, not mine."

"Orlov is an irredeemable alcoholic."

"Today he's a whirlwind."

Victor opened his door and threw up.

"We only order autopsies when there are suspicious circumstances."

"A healthy young woman was dead. If that doesn't make you suspicious, what does?"

"That's enough. I want you here in the office. Where are you now?"

"I don't know. There's a Starbucks on the corner."

"That's no help. Renko, you can resign gracefully or be put out with the trash. Stick with your friend Orlov. You'll sink together."

Five minutes later Arkady sat in a traffic jam on Kutuzovsky while police cleared the way for fleets of government sedans that sped down the center lane and he had time to contemplate the increasing likelihood he was going to be dismissed. Then what? He could cultivate roses. Keep pigeons. Read the great books in their original languages. Exercise. The problem was that being an investigator left a person fit for little else. It was an acquired taste like the Masai's mixture of blood and milk.

He found the Nijinsky Fair invitation that had fallen from the vodka bottle at the trailer and turned it every which way. It wasn't really like a credit card. A little longer and thicker. More like a roulette plaque. The day before he hadn't noticed the existence of the fair and now banners for it seemed to hang on the scaffolding of every construction site in the center of Moscow, NIJINSKY LUXURY FAIR written in silver against a black field.

Arkady found a newsstand at a Metro station. The press covered the fair from different points of view. *Izvestya* approved of its capitalist excess. *Zavtra* detected a Jewish conspiracy. Readers of the more down-to-earth *Gazeta* suggested different luxury items, most having to do with private islands, private castles or sexual enhancement.

To each his dream.

Victor lived in yesterday's version of the future: a spiral of units around a central staircase, each unit a cube of exposed cement combining function and grace. One unit had toppled. It lay on its side, stripped of plumbing and wiring. The city and the historical commission had fought over the building for years because at one time the intelligentsia of Moscow regularly met in the Orlov apartment to debate ideas, read poetry and drink. Esenin, Mayakovsky, Blok had attended at a time when, as Victor put it, poetry wasn't romantic slop. Victor could recite them all. Some people called the building the House of Poets. A cat delicately approached across a yard of empty bottles and dandelions. A pair of kittens watched from a bed of dirty towels.

Victor was refreshed. The shakes had passed and hearing the price of a ticket to Nijinsky Fair snapped him awake.

"Ten thousand dollars to get in the door? Then there'll be free food?"

"I think it's likely. By the way, the prosecutor called. He wants me to resign and he wants you to call Olga an overdose and fold the case."

"Wait. We're in the middle of a homicide case. He's not only fucking you, he's fucking me on the bounce. He's fucking Olga too. I don't mean you, puss." The cat weaved between Victor's feet. "So, what are you going to do?"

"Go to bed."

"No letter of resignation?"

"My heart wouldn't be in it."

"And then?"

"And then I think it would be a shame to miss a night with millionaires. Mix. Show as many people as possible the photo of Olga but be on your good behavior."

"No problem. I can offer them sentiments from Blok: 'John, you bourgeois son of a bitch, you can kiss me where I itch.'" Victor smiled with self-satisfaction. "Poetry for all occasions."

Arkady's apartment was a distinctly bourgeois affair of paneled wood and parquet floors inherited from his father. There were no photos on the walls. No family gallery cn a piano. The women in his life were irretrievably lost. The food in his refrigerator accumulated until he threw it out.

He dropped into bed but slept badly and in a dream found himself in a white room between a stainless-steel table and a laundry bin. In the bin were body parts. It was his task to reassemble the girl he called Olga. The problem was that the bin also contained parts of other women. He recognized each by her color, texture, warmth. No matter what he switched, however, he couldn't complete any single one.

11

★

In the blaze of crystal chandeliers nothing was too expensive or ridiculous. A child's bird rifle that had belonged to Prince Alexei Romanov, once heir to the Russian empire, was offered at $75,000.

An emerald necklace once owned by Elizabeth Taylor: $275,000.

For $25 million, a ride to the International Space Station.

An 1802 Bordeaux left behind by Napoleon as Moscow burned: $44,000.

Models as beautiful and silent as cheetahs lined the red carpet and watched for labels: Bentley, Cartier, Brioni. Arkady, on the other hand, looked as if he had been dressed by a mortician. The disappointment he provoked in women made him feel guilty.

As guests shuffled into the fair Arkady recognized famous athletes, supermodels, marginal celebrities, private bankers and millionaires. Onstage a tennis star giggled through her script. "Welcome to the Nijinsky Fair of luxury goods . . . top social event . . . sponsors like Bulgari, Bentley and the Vaksberg Group. All the proceeds to Moscow children's shelters. Really?"

Their gossip was all about real estate. The Golden Mile was the most expensive real estate in Moscow. In the world, for that matter.

"With an Anglo-American school right around the corner."

"Twenty-four-hour security and roller shut windows."

"Twelve thousand dollars a square meter."

"And a wonderful small church if they would only get rid of the beggars."

Ahead of Arkady a man with sloped shoulders and a pock-marked neck confided to a woman so elegant she had no eyebrows, only pencil lines, that the item he was after was an audience with the pope. "It can't hurt."

Arkady recognized the pilgrim as Aza Baron, formerly Baranovsky, who spent six years in prison for fraud. Upon release, he ran the same scams but called it a hedge fund and became wealthy enough to have his conviction expunged. Voilà! A new name, a new history, a new man. Baron was not the only rags-to-riches story. Arkady spied an Olympic official who, as a youth, beat a rival to death with a cricket bat. Another man's shaved head bore the nicks of a grenade attack, reminders that climbing the ladder of success involved a certain amount of ducking.

A long display case held wristwatches that told time, date, depth, split seconds and time for medication. Up to $120,000. A cello played by Rostropovich. A giant commode employed by Peter the Great.

Security men in Armani black filtered through the crowd. Arkady wondered how to even begin. He imagined tapping Baron on the shoulder and saying, "Excuse me. I am investigating the death of a cheap prostitute and, for all your money, you seemed a likely candidate to ask." Followed by immediate ejection.

A woman on the runway announced, "Fifteen minutes before closing the fair for the night. Thanks to you and your demand for only the best, luxury helps the needy, especially all those innocent girls. Fifteen minutes."

Arkady posed as a man trying to decide between an armored Bentley at $250,000, a Harley-Davidson cruiser studded with diamonds at $300,000 or a Bugatti Veyron as black as a storm cloud at $1.5 million. Security men were definitely coming in Arkady's direction. Someone had checked his name against the VIP list after all. Arkady thought he could live with the social disgrace. He was only angry at himself for failing to show Olga's photo to a single soul.

"What on earth are you doing here?"

It was Anya Rudikova, Arkady's neighbor from the apartment across the hall. A leather satchel hung off her shoulder and a camera around her neck.

To Arkady she was the sort of self-dramatizing journalist who was almost as famous as the people she wrote about. Arkady had seen her on television flushing out a covey of the rich and politically connected. She attacked them and wooed them in equal measure.

"Browsing," Arkady said.

"Do you see anything here that you like?"

"Something that fits my budget. I'm leaning to the Bugatti. One thousand horsepower. Of course, at top speed, you run out of gas in twelve minutes and in fifteen minutes the tires catch fire. That could be exciting."

She pointed toward the mezzanine. "I've been watching you from up there. You have 'police' written all over you."

"And what are you doing here? I thought you were a serious journalist."

"I'm a writer. A writer covers all sorts of stories and this is the social event of the year."

"If you say so." At least the enforcers of Security were backing off. It also explained why Anya was in a black pantsuit and carried a notebook and pen. She should have brought stilts; she was a head shorter than anyone else.

She studied him in turn. "You don't care much for high fashion, do you?"

"I don't know enough about fashion to have an opinion. That's like asking a dog about flying."

"But everyone has a style. A man answers the door wearing little more than a gun? That's a definite fashion statement."

As Arkady remembered, he had been merely shirtless, maybe barefoot when he answered her knock. The odd thing was that he rarely carried a gun. He didn't know why he had picked it up that time, except that he must have heard a scuffle in the hall. Anya had not been frightened then and wasn't now; she seemed to be a small person who enjoyed keeping larger people off balance. "You didn't say how you feel about the rich."

"How rich?" Arkady asked.

"Millionaires. I don't mean small-time millionaires. I mean at least two hundred or three hundred million or more. Or billionaires."

"There are actual billionaires here tonight? That makes me feel less like a dog and more like a speck on the windshield."

"How did you get in?"

"By invitation," Arkady said.

"Invited by whom?"

"I don't know. That's the question."

Something was happening onstage. Anya stood on tiptoe.

"I can't see a thing. Come on." She started up the stairs.

The mezzanine was done up as the diamond mine of the dwarfs in Disney's *Snow White*, which had been huge in Russia, except that here the gems were bottle glass and there was only one dwarf and he was drunk, still wearing a rubber mask and passed out on the floor. Dopey.

Anya motioned Arkady to sit and they joined a man on a cell phone at a front table. A steely bodyguard sat behind and scanned the crowd. Since when did Russians mousse their hair? Arkady felt increasingly inept and unkempt.

"Vaksberg," the man at the table identified himself, and immediately turned his attention back to an argument on the phone. He seemed patient and soft-spoken. He had an expensive tan and a black goatee and was known to the public more fully as Alexander "Sasha" Vaksberg, the Prince of Darkness.

He snapped his phone shut.

"A year ago we had over a hundred billionaires in Moscow. Today there are less than thirty. So it's the best of times, the worst of times and sometimes it's just the shits. It turns out we don't know how to run capitalism. That's to be expected. As it happens, nobody knows how to run capitalism. That was a bad surprise. Cigarette?"

Vaksberg pushed across the table a slim pack that said *Dunhill Personal Blend for Alexander Vaksberg.*

"Vanity cigarettes. I never saw that before." Arkady lit one. "Excellent."

Anya said, "Don't be rude. Sasha arranged this event for homeless children out of his own pocket. Have something to eat. I hear the charlotte russe is delicious."

"After you."

"She wishes," Sasha Vaksberg said. "Our Anyushka is allergic to dairy. Milk is the killer. Show him."

Anya allowed Arkady a glimpse of an emergency wristband on her left arm. What struck Arkady was that Sasha Vaksberg, one of the country's wealthiest men and the evening's host, was being virtually ignored by his peers. Instead he was with a journalist and a policeman, which was a bit of a comedown.

She said, "The scraps will go, of course, to homeless millionaires."

Vaksberg said, "Perhaps so. Someone has to point out to the blockheads in the Kremlin that we have an angry mob; only this mob is made up of the rich. Peasants are hard to rouse, but the rich have expectations."

"Are you talking about violence in the streets?"

"No, no. Violence in the boardroom."

"You two should get along. Investigator Renko always expects the worst," Anya said. "He sleeps with a gun."

"Do you really?" asked Vaksberg.

"No, I'd probably shoot myself."

"But you carry one when you're on duty?"

"On special occasions. There's almost always another way out."

"So you're a negotiator, not a shooter. That's kind of Russian roulette, isn't it? Have you ever guessed wrong?"

"Once or twice."

"You and Anya are a pair. She writes for a fashion journal of mine. Last week the editor asked for a diet piece and she did an article called 'How to Cook Supermodels.'"

"How did the models like it?"

"They loved it. It was about them."

The tennis player returned to the stage and hit a gong. The fair was over. The party was about to begin.

First the floor had to be cleared, which could have been awkward without a curtain to hide the pushing and pulling of display cases. Few guests noticed, however, because a spotlight directed their attention to a dancer in a loose harlequin costume and pointed cap sitting high on a ceiling catwalk, arms and legs dangling, like a puppet placed on a shelf. He moved jerkily, pantomimed a mad passion and, after sobbing from a broken heart, jumped to his fate. Instead of plunging, however, he soared on a single, nearly invisible wire. He seemed to be a creature of the air. It was part illusion. His every move was choreographed with an eye to angles, acceleration and centrifugal force. Shadowy figures on the floor were counterweights, operating in concert to keep the ropes taut so that the flier could freely swing like a pendulum or turn a somersault or fly straight up into a grand jeté.

Mainly it was the flier's daring as he was drawn like a moth from light to light, ending in a series of prodigious leaps à la Nijinsky. The spotlight died on him, and when the houselights went up, the fair had been replaced by a dance floor and tier after tier of tables and booths in rococo white and gold.

A black DJ in a bulging Africa knit cap pulled on headphones, set records on two turntables and made mysterious adjustments on his control panel while he nodded to a beat only he heard. He grinned, just joking, and fed the speakers. Everyone had been so black tie and bloody noble for charity's sake but now the ties were loosened and champagne poured, and in a minute the floor was so crowded that all the dancers could do was writhe in place.

Anya explained that the highest tiers were the most expensive. They were the refuge of older men who, after a shuffle or two, left the floor with honor intact, assured that while the world might be shit, at least the Club Nijinsky was the top of the heap.

Vaksberg said, "This is neutral ground. We have dogs to sniff out bombs and fifty security men to enforce a 'No Guns, No Cameras' policy. We don't want our guests from the Middle East to worry about photos of them with a drink in one hand and a dancer in the other."

"What about Dopey?" Anya asked.

Still in costume, the dwarf had curled up underneath a table and was snoring.

Vaksberg said, "He's breathing and he looks comfortable. Let him be."

Arkady sat back as waiters in white gloves laid a tablecloth and served a chilled bowl of Beluga caviar, warm toast and spoons of mother-of-pearl.

"Young people call Ecstasy a huggy drug because it seems to reduce aggression. They're happy to dance their little heads off in two square centimeters all night long. I can't say enough for it. What do you do for pleasure, Renko?"

"In the winter I ski at Chamonix. In the summertime I sail in Monte Carlo."

"Seriously."

"I read."

"Well, the people at the fair entertain themselves by giving money to charity. In this case to homeless children who are cheated of their childhood and drawn into prostitution, boys and girls. You disapprove?"

"A handout from a billionaire to a starving child? What can be wrong with that?"

Anya said, "Please, the Nijinsky is not a charity. The Nijinsky is a social club for super-rich, middle-aged boys. They only come to table-hop. Their women are supposed to be beautiful, laugh at the men's crude remarks, drink to every toast, endure the clumsy attempts at seduction by their husband's best friends and at the end of the evening be sober enough to undress the old fart and put him to bed."

"And they call me a cynic?" Vaksberg said. "We will continue this conversation but an intermission is coming and I have to go onstage and remind our friends to be generous." He poured champagne for Anya and Arkady. "Five minutes."

Arkady did not understand why Alexander Vaksberg spent even a minute with such an ill-mannered guest. He watched Vaksberg's progress on the dance floor. A billionaire. How much was that? A thousand million dollars. No wonder mere millionaires stepped aside as if an elephant were coming through.

Anya said, "So, you're here to find the person who invited you?"

"Not me. Not exactly."

"This is intriguing."

"We'll see."

He laid on the table a postcard-size photograph of Olga looking straight up from a filthy mattress.

Anya recoiled. "Who is this?"

"I don't know."

"She's dead."

Not all the beauty in the world could mask the fact that no light shone in her eyes, no breath stirred at her lips and she had no objection to the fly examining her ear.

"Why are you showing this picture to me?"

"Because she had a VIP pass to the fair."

"It's possible she's a house dancer. I don't remember her name. They have new dancers here all the time. She's young. Dima, have you seen her?"

The bodyguard peered over Anya's shoulder.

"No. They pay me to watch for troublemakers, not girls."

"And if you find troublemakers?" Arkady was curious.

Dima opened his jacket enough to afford Arkady a glimpse of a matte-black pistol. "A Glock. German engineering never fails."

"I thought no guns were allowed in the club."

Anya said, "Only Sasha and the boys. It's his club. He can write the rules any way he wants."

During an intermission Vaksberg gave a surprisingly heart-felt speech about homeless children. Five to forty thousand lived on the streets of Moscow; there was no accurate count, he said. Most of them were runaways, boys and girls as young as five who preferred life on the street to a household ruined by alcohol, brutality and abuse. Freezing to death in the wintertime.

Squatting in abandoned buildings and surviving on petty theft and restaurant scraps. Vaksberg pointed out volunteers with collection baskets. "Remember, one hundred percent of your donations go to Moscow's invisible children."

Then the records began spinning again and the relentless beat resumed.

"They didn't hear a word," Vaksberg said on his return. "They only know when to clap. I could have been talking to trained seals."

Anya bestowed a kiss on Vaksberg's cheek. "That's why I love you, because you're honest."

"Only around you, Anya. Otherwise, I lie and fabricate as badly as Investigator Renko thinks. I'd be dead if I didn't."

Arkady asked, "What is the problem?"

"Sasha has been receiving threats. I mean more than usual."

"Perhaps he should keep his head down instead of hosting a party with a thousand guests."

Arkady was not about to feel sorry for a billionaire, even one who looked as exhausted as Vaksberg did. He seemed more and more in shadow, his shoulders weary, his smile forced. He was head of the Vaksberg Group, an international chain of casinos and resorts. It seemed to Arkady that Sasha Vaksberg should have been backed by an army of lawyers, accountants, croupiers and chefs rather than a female journalist, an investigator half out the door, a single bodyguard and a drunken dwarf. This was an historical fall. Vaksberg was one of the last of the first oligarchs. He still had a fortune and connections but every day that his operations were shut down his situation deteriorated. It was written on his face.

The houselights dimmed, and when they returned, the Club Nijinsky dancers were on the runway in braids, denim skirts, bare midriffs, short skirts and long socks. Their eyes were outlined with mascara, freckles and rouge applied almost clownishly to their cheeks. In other words, as child prostitutes.

"Ready?" The tennis star had been asked to do the honors with a simpler script in hand.

The dancers straightened up. They might not have been from the Bolshoi but they knew the basic positions of ballet.

"First position!" the tennis player said.

The first girl stood with her feet set heel to heel and her hands on her waist.

Anya said, "I remember this. Every little girl goes through a ballet phase. Then ice skating and then sex."

"Second position!"

The next girl widened her legs and held her arms out at shoulder level.

"Third position!"

The third girl brought her legs together, her right heel ahead of her left. Left arm as before. Right arm lifted in gentle curve overhead.

"Fifth position!"

Legs crossed, left foot touching right instep. Both arms lifted.

Anya asked Vaksberg, "What happened to the fourth position?"

Some in the crowd assumed the tennis player had made a mistake and yelled, "We want the fourth position!"

The call was picked up by the crowd; playfully, but also as a taunt, they stomped their feet and shouted in unison, "We want the fourth! We want the fourth!"

The tennis player burst into tears.

Vaksberg sighed. "It's Wimbledon all over again. I have to deal with this."

A spotlight followed Vaksberg to the stage. On the way Arkady watched the transformation from a defeated man to an energized, take-charge Sasha Vaksberg who bounded up the stairs to the stage and took the microphone. The man had stage presence, Arkady thought. The crowd chanted and he faced them down. He smiled them down.

"Do you want to see the fourth?"

"Yes!"

He shook off his jacket and handed it to the tennis player.

"I can't hear you. Do you really want to see the fourth?"

"Yes!"

"What a feeble choir. You are a disgrace to the city of Moscow. For the last time, do you want to see the fourth position?"

"YES!"

Vaksberg did it deadpan. Right foot pointed out, left foot tucked behind, left hand on the waist and the right arm raised in triumph or grace.

The reaction was shock and delight. Sasha Vaksberg clowning? Hijacking the joke and turning it around until applause started first from the old lions in the upper tiers and then the young crowd on the floor. "Bravo"s and "Encore"s broke out.

Arkady said, "He's a comedian too?"

"He still has a few surprises. When the guests leave the fair tonight, they might talk about a Bugatti for him and a Bulgari for her, but you can be sure that they'll talk about an unworried Sasha Vaksberg."

"He was lucky he knew what to do."

"Luck had nothing to do with it."

That took Arkady a second to decipher.

"You mean it was staged? The entire routine? The tennis player crying? How could he even come up with the idea like that?"

"Because he's Sasha Vaksberg. Let me see the photo again."

Vaksberg took bows. Anya studied the head shot. Smeared mascara and rouge couldn't hide how beautiful the dead girl was and how unblinking, as if she were watching clouds.

"It's Vera," Anya said in a rush. "It's the missing dancer."

"Vera what?"

"I don't know."

"You're a reporter. Maybe it's in your notepad."

"Of course." Anya flipped through the pad. "Here it is, a list of Nijinsky dancers, starting with Vera Antonova." She gave Arkady a second assessment. "Suddenly you sound like an investigator."

12

Zhenya and Maya shared a bag of chips at the all-night café in Yaroslavl Station while he taught her how to use her new cell phone. She tended to shout because there was no wire.

"I can't believe you never used a mobile phone before. Never texted? Videoed?"

"No."

"Where are you from, anyway?"

"You wouldn't know it."

"Try me."

"There's no point."

"Why not?"

"There's no point. So now that I have a telephone, what do I do? I don't know anyone to call."

"You can call me. I put my name at the top of your speed dial."

"Can you take it off?"

"You don't want my number?"

"I don't want anyone's name or number. Can you take it off?"

"Of course. I'll delete it. No problem."

Still it was an awkward moment. He had overstepped again. It was a relief to see a chessboard at the next table. Actually an electronic chess game. The man hunched over it was about fifty years old, with a red nose peeking out of a gray beard. In a virtually unintelligible British accent he ordered another gin. Zhenya noticed that the game's level of difficulty was set at Intermediate. It was painful to see a grown man bested by a motherboard.

Zhenya dropped his voice and told Maya, "We're running a little low on pocket money. Give me five minutes alone."

"I'll be in the main hall. Don't call your friend the investigator."

"Five minutes."

He waited until she left before he paid any attention to his neighbor. He seemed eccentric, vaguely professorial, pretty much what Zhenya expected in an Englishman.

"Hard game?"

"Pardon?"

"Chess."

"Well, it certainly is when you're playing against open space, a vacuum, so to speak. Very disorienting."

"I know what you mean. I have the same machine. It beats me all the time."

"You do play, then. This is very lucky. Look, if your train is not departing soon, perhaps we could squeeze in a game. Do you know speed chess?"

"Blitz? I've played it once or twice."

"Five minutes' sudden death. The chessboard has a game clock. Are you up for it?"

"If you'd like."

"Your girlfriend wouldn't mind?"

"She's fine."

"Henry." They shook hands as Zhenya switched tables.

"Ivan."

There was an art to barely winning. Henry brought out his queen too soon, didn't protect his rooks, let his knights stagnate on the side of the board. Zhenya made some judicious blunders of his own and didn't corner the Englishman's king until there had been satisfactory bloodletting on both sides.

Henry was good-natured and full of winks. "Youth will be served. However, it's a different game when there's money on the line. Yes, it is. Then there are consequences. Have you ever done that? Faced the consequences?"

"Sure. I won ten dollars once."

"Then you're practically professional. How about it, then? Another game?"

Zhenya won with the stakes at ten dollars, again at twenty. Henry set up the pieces. "How about a hundred?"

Yegor slid into the seat next to Maya and whispered, "I hear you're looking for a baby."

Maya stiffened as if there were a snake at her feet. Suddenly it was reassuring to be surrounded by the waiting hall's army of travelers, sleeping or not.

"Where did you hear that?"

"You've asked half the people in this station. Word gets around. A baby? That's a real shame. That's really sick. I'd kill someone who did that. I really would. If I can help, just say the word. Seriously."

If Yegor had seemed large in the fluorescent glare of the tunnel, he seemed to expand in the dusk of the waiting hall.

"The problem is that people don't believe you. They don't think you had a baby. I know you did because you kind of fucked up my beautiful white silk scarf with your mother's milk and all. It was an accident, I know. Don't worry about it."

She stayed mute although she couldn't say that she was to-tally surprised to see Yegor. She had half expected him ever since he placed his hands on her in the tunnel.

Yegor said, "I suppose Genius is on the case. Genius is the smartest guy I know. What's the capital of Madagascar? Card tricks? That sort of thing. The problem with Genius is that he lives in a world of his own. I don't think he knows ten people. You couldn't have picked anyone more useless if you tried. You'll never find your baby. But I can."

She had to ask.

"How?"

"You buy her. That's what we do, the boys and me. Protect things or bring them back. Last night with the Canadian, that was more of a romp, like. Unusual. We hear all the rumors, all the news, and we assess and react. For example, you were asking the conductor about Auntie Lena. We'd track her down. We're a network like the police but less expensive. You don't want to end up in the courts, do you? They'd send your baby to America and you'd never see it again."

"What about Zhenya's friend, the investigator?"

"He's a wreck. I wouldn't let him near a baby."

"How much? What would it cost?" She didn't believe a word he said, but it wouldn't hurt to know.

"Well, in this situation every second counts. We'd commit all our resources full-time right away. To start, five hundred dollars. After negotiations and satisfactory delivery, more like five thousand. But I guarantee you'll get your baby."

"I don't have that much money. I don't have any money."

"No friends or family to borrow from?"

"No."

"Last night you said you had a brother."

"I don't."

"That's too bad. Maybe . . ."

"Maybe what?"

"Maybe we could work out an arrangement."

"What sort of arrangement?"

Yegor's voice went hoarse and he leaned close enough for his beard to tickle her ear.

"You work it off."

"Doing what?"

"Whatever the customer wants. It's not like you're a virgin."

"It's not like I'm a prostitute either."

"Don't be angry. I was trying to do you a favor. It must drive you crazy imagining what they're doing to your baby. Are they feeding her? Changing her nappies? Is she still alive?" He got to his feet. "I'll be back at this spot in two hours in case you change your mind."

"Rot in hell."

Yegor sighed like a man who had done his best. "It's your baby."

In the middle of the game Zhenya wondered about Maya. Sooner or later her wandering would catch the attention of the militia, perhaps of the lieutenant she had outraced when Zhenya first saw her, when she was a flash of red hair in the crowd. If she were stopped without some form of identification, she would be put in a juvenile holding cell where she could be held for a year before seeing a judge or placed in a children's shelter where she might be held even longer. It occurred to him that she might not be wandering at all. She could be headed for the Metro with her razor.

Meanwhile Henry's game turned sly and accrued small advantages, saddling Zhenya with doubled pawns and forcing the unequal swap of a bishop for a knight.

"Check!"

Zhenya was lost in anxious reverie. He imagined Maya on a Metro platform. It was rush hour and the pressure of the crowd had forced her over the "Stand Clear" warning. Being a country girl, what would she know about pickpockets or perverts? Women were groped, especially at rush hour. Accidents happened. It was easy to imagine. The clock over the tunnel counting the seconds until the next train. A breeze and a halo of head beams approaching. The crowd surging forward; no one made it easy for passengers getting off the train. An indistinct flurry of motion. Shouts and screams.

Henry repeated, "Check!"

As Zhenya emerged from daydreams the flesh-and-blood Maya appeared at the buffet, her mood hidden in the shadow of her hood. He was relieved; at the same time he couldn't help but wonder where she had been. Also, with his first good look at the board, he was unhappy to find that with less than two minutes on his game clock, he was on the brink of losing to Henry, who grinned in his beard, performed his tics and winks and said in perfectly native Russian, "Never hustle a hustler."

Maya said, "I thought you were looking for the baby. You're still playing chess."

"You knew I was." Zhenya concentrated on the board.

"I left half an hour ago. You didn't look anywhere?"

"Just let me finish this."

"Can we go now?" Maya asked.

"I need five minutes."

"That's what you said before."

"Five more minutes is all." Zhenya could save the game. He saw escape and beyond, a combination that was all green lights.

Maya swept the pieces off the board. Plastic pieces bounced and rolled under tables and along the buffet counter. The eyes of the café turned to Maya.

"Can we go now?"

"After he pays up," said Henry.

Zhenya grimly picked pieces off the floor. Losing money didn't bother him as much as being publicly humiliated at what was essentially his place of business. He had been a prodigy; now he was pathetic. Also he was confused. He was the one with every right to be upset; yet it was Maya who radiated fury and contempt.

On their way to the Peter the Great, Zhenya again and again considered sending her away with, "Good luck. You're on your own." However, he didn't actually voice the words, not even when she demanded the combination to the touch pad at the casino's rear door.

"So we don't get in each other's way," she said.

"What do you mean?"

"I mean you don't have to help me anymore."

"I don't mind." Which was both true and a lie.

"No, you play your games and I'll do what I came for."

Zhenya remembered that before he admitted Maya into his life, everything was smooth sailing. He was a winner. He hustled with single-minded focus, was a respected member of the Three Stations community and had a luxurious casino all to himself. He was the acknowledged Genius. Everything had been turned upside down. Now he was a loser about to lose possession of the one place he considered his own. At the back door of the casino he gave her what she wanted. She punched in the code herself to be sure.

"You don't trust me?" Zhenya said.

"Maybe you'll lie to me, maybe you won't."

"Thank you. What are you so angry about?"

"My baby is missing and you play chess."

"To get money for us."

"For us? You mean for you—so you can play more games. I'm better off on my own. All you know is money. You're just a hustler."

"And you're nothing but a bitch."

That made her flinch. The word felt like a good weapon, one that a man could use over and over.

13

Maya had been the youngest prostitute at the club. She was special, off the menu, for trusted members only.

Her room was pink and on the shelves were rows of dolls with stitched smiles and button eyes, the way they would be in a girl's bedroom when Daddy came to say, "One last kiss."

She loathed dolls.

One good thing about her room was that it looked out on a two-lane road with a bus shelter and streetlamp. The shelter was strangely reassuring and at night the lamp cast a glow like embers.

The club was set back and shared a wide parking lot with a garage and a motel, a skid mark in the middle of nowhere, yet there was never a lack of customers. Some as rough and unshaven as wild boars. The old arrived like pilgrims at Lourdes, on legs wrapped in varicose veins, carrying swollen bellies, suffering from high blood pressure and limp dicks and hoping for a cure from her, a child prostitute. Often the ones who played daddy ended up in tears. They were the best tippers, but in the end they all squeezed the breath out of her.

At school she was half asleep, which teachers ascribed to anemia, probably due to her first period. She made no friends, no one whose home she might visit or who would expect to visit her own. On doctor's orders she didn't engage in sports or after-school activities. A car delivered her at the first bell in the morning and picked her up as soon as school let out, which gave Maya four hours to eat dinner and finish her homework before the first customers arrived.

Otherwise, she was an average girl.

The club manager, Matti, fancied himself a Tom Jones lookalike, down to ruffled shirts and sentimental songs. As a proud Finn, he upheld his country's prejudices: Russians were incompetent drunks while Finns were competent drunks. This declaration invariably led to drinking bouts with friends in the militia when they came for their protection money. If he lost, Matti offered a free lay with any girl except Maya. His voice would drop reverently and he would say, "Delicate goods."

When Maya tried to slit her wrist in the tub, Matti asked, "What is the matter with you? Why do you hurt yourself? Don't you know how good you have it here, like a princess? Don't you know people love you? Don't tell the other girls but you're making more money than anyone else. It's like the *Mona Lisa*. This famous museum in Paris has a thousand works of art but all anyone wants to see is one painting. You can't even get in that room it's so crowded. The same with you. And you've got all that money piling up in safekeeping."

"How much?"

"I can't say offhand. I haven't counted it lately. A lot."

"Why don't you take the money and let me go?"

"That's up to your parents because you're underage. They're always looking out for your best interest. I'll call them."

"Can I talk to them?"

"If they want. They're the ones running the show. I'm just the guy catching the shit. In the meantime I want you to wear these." Matti tied red ribbons around her wrists. "And stop smoking. Good girls don't smoke."

She crossed the road to look at the bus shelter. It had been built during a period of optimism, and although the paint had faded and holes had been mysteriously punched through the wall, Maya could still make out the faint outline of a rocket ship lifting off the ground, aspiring to more.

The bus route had been closed for years. The shelter was mainly used now as a pissoir and message center: GO FUCK YOUR-SELF, I FUCKED YOUR MOTHER, HEIL HITLER, OLEG SUCKS COCK. The walls were still solid enough to collect rays of the sun on cool days and stay cool on warm. Maya sat on the bench and fantasized that it was a warm lap.

No one worried that she was going anywhere. The road was straight and what little traffic there was blew by like a jet stream. Once in a while an army truck stopped at the club, but Matti never let the soldiers in because they were too loud and too poor.

There was nothing else.

They could have been on Mars.

Despite her small size, Maya didn't show that she was pregnant until her fourth month.

"You knew," Matti said. "You knew when you missed your periods. You knew then and now we're fucked. Well, we'll just have to get rid of it."

"If the baby goes, I go."

She started slicing her wrist.

Matti said, "Okay, okay. But when this baby comes into the world, you have to give it up. Find someone suitable. No one comes to a brothel to hear a baby crying."

"Very cute, very cute, very cute," Matti said when the baby came. "Did you find someone suitable?"

"No," Maya said.

"Did you ask?"

"No. Her name is Katya."

"I don't want to know. She can't stay."

"She'll be quiet."

The baby was swaddled and asleep in a basket next to Maya's bed. Blankets, nappies, cans of talcum powder and jars of petroleum jelly filled a second basket.

"So you've got a system, fucking with one hand and nursing with the other? You know what I've been told to do." Matti opened his pocketknife. "It will just take a second and it will be just like popping a balloon."

"Then you'll have to kill me too. You'll have two bodies, not one."

"You don't even know who the father is. Someone you rode bareback with. It's probably got AIDS and a dozen other diseases."

"Don't touch my baby. Close the knife."

"You were going to give it up. You agreed."

"Close the knife."

"You're making this very hard. You don't know these people."

"Who?"

"These people. They don't make bargains with little girls. They don't make bargains with anyone."

"Then I'll leave. You're holding my money. It's 'a lot,' you said."

"That was before you got yourself pregnant. That's lost revenue, plus room and board. Then medical bills, clothes, taxes, various expenses. After subtracting the money I was keeping for you, you owe the club eighty-one thousand, four hundred and fifty dollars."

"Eighty-one thousand, four hundred and fifty?"

"I can show it to you itemized."

"Did you talk to my parents?"

"Your mother says you made your bed, you lie in it. You'll have to work it off."

She followed Matti's eyes. "Have I been sold?"

He slapped her and left a hot imprint of his hand on her cheek.

"You're a bright girl. You know better than to ask that sort of question. Don't ever ask that question again."

Maya retreated to the bus shelter. The figure $81,450 kept racing through her mind but the shelter calmed her. Sunday business was slow and she and Katya sat in the shelter for hours. All a three-week-old baby did was sleep and all Maya did was watch her sleep. It amazed Maya that out of her had come anyone so perfect, so completely formed and translucent that she glowed. Maya saw Matti watching from a club window. The sky, the road, the lamp, the girl, the baby. Everything was the same, day after day, except that the baby was growing.

Matti got Maya alone in the club lounge, a den of red velvet settees and erotic statues. It was eleven in the morning and he looked and smelled as if he had spent the night in a bottle of vodka.

He asked, "Do you know the difference between a Russian and a Finn?"

"A competent drunk and an incompetent drunk. You told me before."

"No, princess, it's thoroughness. See, you don't know who you're dealing with. These people don't do things by halves.

They have clubs like this around the world. And girls like you around the world. Girls who get ideas about leaving before they work off their debt." He showed her a photograph. "Can you imagine this was a pretty girl?" He showed her another photo. "Can you call that a face? Go ahead, study them. Maybe you'll learn something."

Maya rushed to the bar sink and threw up.

"So you know." Matti swayed on his feet. "To these people you're no one special. To them you're just a bitch who talks too much."

They came the next day, two men in coveralls and boots in an ancient Volvo station wagon. Maya immediately labeled them "the Catchers." She was ready, with Katya in one basket and nappies in another, as if they were setting off on a day trip. The men would have thrown her and the baby in the rear of the wagon at once if their car hadn't rattled and limped for the last kilometer with a flat tire and a hole in the muffler. When the mechanic at the garage said that he could replace both the tire and muffler in half an hour, the Catchers decided to have lunch in the air-conditioned comfort of the lounge.

The question was what to do with Maya. They couldn't keep her in the car while it was on the lift and they didn't want her mixing with her coworkers; in fact, the Catchers didn't want her back in the club at all. It was Matti who suggested the bus shelter, where Maya would be in plain sight and serve as an object lesson. The men looked up and down the road and at the waist-high grass around the shelter and returned to their cabbage and sour cream.

Maya herself was relieved to be in the bus shelter. It was her special place. The rest of the world had receded and left her with only Katya and the trilling of a million insects. She had never really listened to them before. She had never prayed before.

"Good news and bad news," the mechanic reported to the

men in the lounge. "The new tire is on but we are having a small problem with the muffler. The bolts were rusted for good. I used a lubricant, ratchet and wrenches. Next I'll use a hacksaw. I might need another twenty minutes."

"You might need a gun stuck up your ass."

Maya decided that she would keep the baby alive as long as possible but that, if need be, she would kill it herself rather than let it be tortured.

"Cheers!" Matti raised a glass of vodka. The Catchers ignored their glasses although he had filled them to the brim. "No? What if you take turns? A single Finn versus two Russians? Those are fair odds."

"Fuck you," said the Catchers, and they lifted their vodkas.

The sound of an engine overlapped insect song and a bus emerged from the heat waves of the highway.

"Just a tiny one." Matti poured the next vodka only to the brim.

It was an army bus of recruits, all Sir Galahads when they saw a girl sitting at the shelter.

The Catchers bolted from the lounge. "You said there was no bus service. Now here's a bus and our car is up on a fucking lift."

"There is no bus service," Matti said. "There is an army camp nearby. Sometimes a bus or truck of theirs rolls through."

The bus doors opened and Maya boarded tentatively, as if the bus and soldiers might dissolve at her touch.

The Catchers ran across the parking lot. One drew a gun but the other told him to put it away.

Matti motioned, go, go.

At the start Maya endured a hundred questions. After a while the soldiers relaxed in the glow of a good deed and she rode to town unharried.

An outdoor market surrounded the train station. Maya's money was in her room at the club, but her tips from the night before were more than enough to buy two canvas bags, blue jeans, a secondhand leather jacket and a dye job at a station salon while the women on the staff admired Katya. Only then, transformed, did Maya approach the ticket counter and purchase an overnight ticket to Moscow. Hard class. She had never been to Moscow but she believed it was a good place to hide.

"Miracles are happening. Our luck has changed," she told the baby as the train pulled out. Maya laughed from exhilaration. She had been entrusted with the most precious item in the world and she had successfully protected it. From this point on, everything was going to be different.

Katya stirred. Before she started crying, Maya went out to the vestibule at the end of the car and put the baby to her breast. Once the baby's first urgent scrambling settled down, Maya allowed herself a cigarette. She would not have minded if the moment went on forever, watching fields shine in the moonlight, smuggling her baby into the world.

Maya didn't hear a drunken soldier join her until the door clicked shut behind him.

That was ages ago, Maya thought. Two days at least. Well, bitches were as bitches did. She closed her eyes until Zhenya was asleep, then she took the last money in his day pack and left the casino.

14

★

Arkady called Victor from the dancers' dressing room and told him that the murder victim they called Olga had been identified as Vera Antonova, age nineteen, a student at Moscow State University, and suggested that since this was the detective's case, he might want to come by the Club Nijinsky and take part in the investigation.

"I can't leave. I'm getting a tattoo."

"Now? At this hour?"

"No problem. The parlor is open all night."

Arkady didn't know what to say. He paced back and forth in the narrow, brightly lit comma of space that was afforded dancers. A makeup counter was littered with used tissues, jars of foundation, powder and rouge, cold cream, lipstick and mascara. It was hard to imagine six women squeezing into the room, let alone changing from one costume to another.

Victor said, "I'm sober, if that's what you're wondering."

Arkady still didn't know what to say. He noticed snapshots of boyfriends and family wedged into mirrors; none seemed to have any connection to Vera Antonova.

"Who identified her?" Victor asked.

"A journalist who writes about the club scene, then several other people. It seems that besides being a student, she was a dancer at the Nijinsky."

"Too bad."

"But why are you getting a tattoo?"

"You can't hang out in tattoo parlors without getting something. By the way, Zurin called looking for you about a letter of resignation that he expected. He said that as far as the prosecutor's office is concerned, you have been suspended. You are no longer an active investigator. Any pretense otherwise and he will have you detained."

"Arrested?"

"Decapitated, if he had a choice."

"When can you get over here? You're the one who always says the detective leads and the investigator follows." As he talked, Arkady rapidly opened and shut drawers. He saw Ecstasy in the form of candies, clear capsules and green peas, yes. Clonidine or ether, no. With so many mirrors reflecting each other, he seemed to share the room with multiple desperate men with lank hair and eyes deep as drains, the sort of figure who might wander the streets on a rainy night and cause people to roll up their car windows and jump the traffic light.

Victor was saying, "You can't rush an artist. I'll call you in the morning."

"Does the tattoo hurt?"

"It stings a little."

"Good."

★

Isa Spiridona was graceful and gray. Arkady remembered her from the Bolshoi, briefly as a prima ballerina before she was injured. He would have thought she might continue as a ballet mistress, teaching young dancers to elevate their leg or their elbow thus and so. Instead she was a choreographer at the Club Nijinsky with a desk crammed between a rack of costumes and stacks of CDs and DVDs arranged around a balsa-wood model of the club interior that showed runways, dance floor and mini-stages. Arkady poked it with his finger.

"Where are we in this model?"

"I don't discuss any of the club's operations. Please don't touch."

"I've always loved models." He stooped for a better view. "Does the service elevator go up and down?"

"No, it's not a dollhouse. Don't touch, please."

"Where did you say we are?"

"Here." She pointed to the third level; there were five levels altogether. "Have you shown this picture to any of the dancers?"

"Yes."

"Without coming to me first? Dancers are children. I don't want them sobbing before the audience is out the door. Stay away from the girls. If you have questions, call me tomorrow and I'll make some time for you."

Tomorrow had arrived hours ago, Arkady thought. As for time, he only had until Zurin caught up with him.

Spiridona's phone rang and she sat to take the call.

"No, I'm not alone. There's an investigator here, but he's leaving . . . totally useless and scaring the girls . . . Wait a second. He's not bright enough to take a hint." She gave Arkady a wave of dismissal. "Can't you see I'm working?"

"So am I. May I have Vera's photograph, please?"

"Oh." Spiridona found it in her hand and thrust it at Arkady. "Now will you go? I can't believe you showed this to my dancers."

"But I didn't show them this."

He dug into his jacket and gave Spiridona a different photograph and watched her gaze swim over the filthy mattress, Vera's half-stripped body, the butterfly tattoo resting on her hip.

Spiridona hung up. "I don't understand."

Arkady said, "Neither do I."

"Dear God, how could this happen?" She dropped the picture as if it were a spider. "Who could do this to her?"

"I don't know." He described the circumstances in which the girl was found: "Dressed like a prostitute, tattooed like a prostitute, on a prostitute's bed, carrying a prostitute's knockout powder."

"I can't explain it. It isn't the Vera I knew."

"Who was?"

"A free spirit, you could say."

"Sexually free?"

That drew a wistful smile. "Everyone is different. In a ballet company there are three or four genders. Vera was popular from the first and men and women were drawn to her like bears to honey. She was ambitious. She could have had any of a dozen millionaires, so why would she be selling herself at Three Stations?"

"Do you know who those men are?"

"I can give you a list but it would be incomplete and out-of-date. She was a fickle girl. She roomed at the university. You should talk to her roommate there."

"What was she studying?"

"Languages. Foreign affairs."

Arkady was impressed. Foreign affairs was usually reserved for the elite. It was hard for Arkady himself to believe but he had once been a member of Moscow's "Gilded Youth," when dinosaurs ruled the earth.

"How did she get on with the other dancers?"

"Fine."

"No particular enemies?"

"No."

"No particular friends?"

"No."

"You interviewed her before taking her on as a dancer?"

"Of course. This is not the Bolshoi. I am more of an orna-
ment than a teacher and the girls do more or less what they want.
But this is also the Club Nijinsky. People expect a different wild
and crazy theme every week but also, for the amount of money
they're paying, a touch of culture. Not too much, maybe ten seconds' worth. Some pirouettes or a *tableau vivant*. Girls line up
to be a Nijinsky dancer, to have all those wealthy men admiring
you, enamored of you." She lit a cigarette and dramatically ex-
haled smoke that twisted into arabesques. "Worshipping you."

"Is her family in Moscow?"

"Her parents died in the terrorist bombing of the Metro.
Her brother died in the army. He hung himself."

"Why?"

"He was gay."

Which said quite enough. Hazing new recruits in the Red
Army was routine. For "homos," torture.

"When did this happen?"

"Around New Year's. She was upset but nothing unusual.
She was a focused person, that's why this"—she indicated the
photo of Vera in the trailer—"makes no sense at all."

"Did she dress well?"

"Nothing cheap or shoddy."

"But no diamonds."

"No."

"So tonight you had your dancers pose in all five basic ballet positions except the fourth. Was that supposed to be Vera?"

"Yes."

"Why didn't someone take her place?"

"Vera often showed up at the last moment. I admit I made allowances for her. The girl was carrying a full scholastic load. I respected that."

"Did you report her missing?"

"If she had been gone a week. She led an active social life. That's part of being young, isn't it? The energy?"

"Did she ever use drugs?"

"None of my girls do or they're dismissed immediately. I won't have it."

"When was the last time you saw her?"

"Thursday afternoon at rehearsal."

"The exact hours?"

"From two to five. We only rehearse twice a week because, as I told you, the dancers for the most part create their own choreography. All I ask is that they don't fall off the runway."

"Her mood was . . ."

"Upbeat always."

"Please remind me, the theme for this weekend was . . ."

"Abused children. Girls in particular. I put together costumes that mixed different elements, such as Lolita, Hello Kitty, Japanese schoolgirls and the ballet phase in little girls."

"I saw it. There seemed to be something missing."

"What do you mean?"

"Whatever Vera would have represented. You can look at the photograph if that will help you remember."

Her eyes darted as briefly as possible to the photo.

"I suppose you could say she looked like a prostitute."

"Did the dancers choose which costume to wear or did you assign them?"

"I assigned them. I saw them as an ensemble."

"Do you recognize what Vera was wearing when she was killed? The skirt, the top, the boots?"

"One can't be certain."

"What is your first impression?"

"It does look like the costume."

"That you selected for her?"

"Yes, but they weren't supposed to take the costumes home. Why would she wear it at night anyplace as dangerous as Three Stations?"

"Has she recently mentioned any travel plans?"

"None." Isa Spiridona corrected herself. "None that I know of."

"Can you think of anyone who might wish her harm? A former lover? A jealous colleague?"

"No. The career of a dancer is brief enough. One wrong step, one fall, one trip."

"As distinct from a fall?"

"Yes. That's why dancers are so superstitious." Her attention returned to the photo. "The tattoo is new."

"Since when?"

"Two weeks."

"Thank you. That helps with the time line."

Spiridona pursed her lips. "You are kind to put it that way."

Arkady gave her his card. "In case you recall anything else. It's probably best to call my cell phone. I'm never in my office."

Leaving Madame Spiridona's office, Arkady had to press against the wall as three Chinese dressed in black and carrying loops of cable hustled out of the service elevator. The elevator sat there, doors open, practically an invitation. Arkady entered and pressed five.

When the doors opened, he stepped into a world painted black. Platforms, catwalks, rails and hooded lights designed to disappear. Below was the world of color, where beams of light dyed the air red, blue and green. A globe glittered and spun as dancers waved to an endless pulsating beat. From five floors above, it all seemed virtually remote.

Petrouchka sat on a middle catwalk looking sad as only a clown could be. He idly kicked his legs over the side and ignored Arkady's arrival.

"I know why you come up here," Arkady said.

"Why?"

"To be alone."

Although his costume was baggy, it couldn't hide the clown's muscularity any more than greasepaint could hide his condescension. "That's right, and yet you're here."

"You're the man who flies on the wire," Arkady said.

"You're still here."

"Well, I've never seen a stage from this angle before." As his eyes adjusted, he saw a spaceship, a chandelier, a baby carriage—props of yesterday's entertainment, suspended from the ceiling. On the catwalk next to Petrouchka lay a harness and neatly coiled wire and rope.

"What will it take to get rid of you?"

"A few questions," Arkady said.

"About what?"

"Flying."

"I don't think it's for you."

"Why not?"

"Well, there are two kinds of fliers. A two-wire flier is hauled around like a suitcase, safe and slow. The one-wire flier goes where he wants as fast as he wants. This is a one-wire rig." He looked Arkady up and down, "You are definitely a two-wire man."

"You mean a man on the ground at the other end of the wire?"

"A man. Or a sandbag."

"What is your name?" Arkady asked.

"Petrouchka."

"You're still in character."

"Always. The same as you. You are a policeman, aren't you?"

"How did you guess?"

"You've got that 'doormat of the world' look."

"You think so?"

"Absolutely."

"Did you know Vera Antonova?"

"I don't know. Who was she?"

"A dancer here at the club."

"No, I'm new here myself."

"You're not from Moscow?"

Petrouchka lit a cigarette. The match was wood, and rather than blow out the flame, he let it drop into the canopy of floodlights.

"Some clown," said Arkady. "Do you want this place to burn?"

"For every question, a match. That's the game."

"Are you crazy?"

"See, that's two." The clown struck another match and let it drift down toward coiffures, bare shoulders, décolletages. Arkady knew it was unlikely any live flame would get that far, but all it took for a disaster was one person screaming "Fire!"

"Will you stop?"

"And another." Petrouchka struck a third match and let the flame get good and set before letting it drop. "More?"

Arkady said, "Vera Antonova is dead. That's not a question."

The clown didn't answer. At least he didn't strike a match, Arkady thought.

"She was a beautiful girl. That's not a question either. I have her picture."

The clown got to his feet and said, "I'll show you how this works."

He took a meter's length of nylon rope, climbed the rail and reached up to two pulleys above his head. His sense of balance was phenomenal. Standing on a rail in the semidark, he ran the rope through the pulleys, made a loop in one end and handed the other to Arkady. "Hang on," he told Arkady.

"Why?"

"You're my counterweight." The clown slipped a foot into the loop and stepped off the catwalk. He plunged until the rope snapped taut in Arkady's hands. The rope was slippery and all Arkady could do was play it out until Petrouchka was gracefully delivered onto the dance floor. As his descent was noted by guests they made way and applauded. He gave Arkady a farewell wave.

Arkady felt like a fool and, worse, that he had missed something important. He didn't know where but he was convinced he had met Petrouchka before, although not in greasepaint or a clown's costume. A man elbows you in the Metro and you catch only a glimpse of his face, but the memory stays with you like a bruise.

15

★

At 5 a.m., while diehards stayed for the last dance, the last toast, the last laugh of the night, Arkady emerged from the Club Nijinsky to find the city in the path of a thunderstorm. Gusts of wind stirred litter on the street and fat drops of rain pinged off car roofs and windshields

Arkady had parked blocks away rather than submit the Lada to the gibes of parking attendants. Victor had put pots and pans inside the car in case of rain.

A man and woman hustling to beat the storm brushed by. Another couple ran past, the woman in bare feet to spare the high-heeled shoes she held in her hand. One pair of footsteps synchronized with his and he found Dima the bodyguard at his side. The Glock hung openly on Dima's shoulder.

While Dima gave Arkady a pat-down, a Mercedes S550 limousine caught up. A side window slid down and Sasha Vaksberg begged a few more minutes of Arkady's time.

Arkady was flattered but now he wished he'd brought a gun.

Vaksberg and Anya shared the rear seat with a red-and-white Spartak athletic bag. Arkady and Dima took jump seats facing rear in a conference arrangement. As the car pulled away Arkady felt its extra weight and stiffness of armor, bulletproof glass and run-flat tires. The driver must have pushed a button because the doors had silently locked.

"Could we have some heat back here, Slava? Our friend is a little damp from the rain." Vaksberg turned to Arkady. "So, what did you think of our Club Nijinsky?"

"Unforgettable."

"And the women?" he asked. "Did you find them tall and beautiful enough?"

"Amazons," Arkady said.

Anya said, "It's not by chance. Girls flock to Moscow with romantic ambitions of being models or dancers and Moscow turns them into escorts and whores. We wax them and pluck them and inflate their breasts like balloons. In short, we turn them into freaks of beauty."

"Where are we going?" Arkady asked.

"An excellent question," Vaksberg said. "We could go to my casino on the Arbat. No, that's been closed. Or the casino at Three Stations. No, that's been closed too. In fact, all my casinos have been closed. I was taking in a million dollars a day. Now, thanks to our judo master in the Kremlin, I'm just paying rent."

Arkady appreciated how Vaksberg avoided saying Putin's name. "Are you down to your last five hundred million?"

"You don't have much sympathy."

"Not a great deal. So we're just going to drive?"

"And have a conversation. Am I correct, Anya?"

"I hope so."

Rain drummed on the roof. Sitting backward, looking through heavy rain and tinted glass, Arkady lost track of where he was.

Vaksberg said, "I may be many things but I am not a hypocrite. When the dear old Soviet Union broke up, I made a great deal of money. It was like creating a new jigsaw puzzle out of old pieces. Granted, we took advantage where we could. What great fortune did not at the start? The Medicis', the Rothschilds', the Rockefellers'? You don't think they all had bloody hands at the beginning?"

"So you're aspiring to the elite."

"The very best. But fortune is a bubble unless the state accepts the rights of private property. In an emerging nation—and Russia, believe me, is an emerging nation—that bubble can be easily popped. Who would want to do business in a land where rich men are poisoned or put in cages and shipped to Siberia? We thought we were the darlings of the Kremlin. Now we're all on a little list."

"Who is on the list?" Arkady was curious.

"Us, the so-called oligarchs. We were the idiots who put this lizard in power. Our lizard turned out to be Tyrannosaurus rex. I used to have more than twenty venues in Moscow. Now every single one is dark except the Club Nijinsky. I have chefs, floor managers, croupiers, better than a thousand people I pay every week simply to stand by. The Nijinsky is my last toehold. They will use any excuse to drive me out, and a scandal about a dead girl would do it."

"Too bad. I think she was killed."

"In that case, I want whoever did it."

"Wouldn't that create a scandal?"

"Not if it's done right, not if it's managed properly."

"I don't like where this is going," Anya said.

Vaksberg leaned forward. Close up, he looked tired, skin rough as parchment and beard and brows dyed inky black, an aging devil relying on his makeup. He asked Arkady, "What are you doing here? You're investigating by yourself? I don't see anyone else."

"I'm assisting a detective who's following other leads."

"As an investigator?"

"Yes."

Vaksberg put it gently. "I talked to Zurin."

"Prosecutor Zurin? At this hour?" Arkady had to admit that that possibility had not occurred to him.

"Yes. I apologized for calling him so late but I have never talked to a man more eager to unburden himself. He said that you had no reason to investigate anything because you were under suspension. In fact, he described you as a self-aggrandizing liar with a history of violence. Was Prosecutor Zurin correct? Are you under suspension?"

"Not yet."

"But soon. Zurin was full of information. Did you ever actually shoot a prosecutor?"

"That was a long time ago."

"Have you been shot yourself?"

"Years ago."

"In the brain?"

"In the head."

"Now, there's a fine distinction. Described by Prosecutor Zurin, you are an unstable, brain-damaged impostor. Practically a rabid dog."

"Is that what you are?" Anya asked Arkady.

"No."

Sometimes the sound of the rain was overwhelming, as if a flood bearing houses, trees, cars was at their heels. Dima followed the exchange with his finger on the trigger. Arkady sympathized. People thought that one of the advantages of being fabulously rich was that you could shoot up the soft interior of a bulletproof car—shred the upholstery and soak it in blood— but at close quarters, with the armor and all, ricochets could be fierce.

Arkady said, "Leave the country until it's safe to come back. You're the head of a worldwide organization. I'm sure you have moved enough money overseas to have a fresh croissant and orange juice every morning."

"They've confiscated my passport," Vaksberg said. "I'm trapped."

"Never a good sign," Arkady had to agree.

"I need my passport so that I travel freely and conduct business. Also I insist on being able to return and defend my interests. For that I need intelligent, trustworthy people around me."

"I'm sure you have candidates by the score."

"But they're not here and the ones who are here are intimidated. Why do you think we're meeting here and being half drowned? My office is bugged. My car and phones are compromised. I need someone who knows the law but isn't held back by it. In a sense, Zurin gave you the highest possible recommendation. An investigator who killed a prosecutor. My, my."

Slava steered around a barricade of orange tubs and let the car coast up an unfinished highway overpass, an elegant four-lane curve of concrete that terminated in midair. There were no cement mixers or generators or any other sign of recent activity. The car came to a halt ten meters short of the end of the ramp.

Slava unlocked the doors.

"You want us to get out?" Arkady asked.

Sasha Vaksberg said, "We have umbrellas. You're not afraid of a little rain, are you?"

Anya said, "I'm staying here."

"You will have to forgive me," Vaksberg told Arkady. "I'm paranoid, but when you've been betrayed as many times as I have, you will be paranoid too. It's a sixth sense."

Dima opened an umbrella for Vaksberg as he stepped out of the car. Arkady declined an umbrella and walked up the ramp to a 360-degree view of the city. The lights of the city were as subdued as banked coals. Lightning played in the clouds and it occurred to Arkady that an overpass bristling with steel rebars might not be the safest place to be when great electrical imbalances were being redressed. If he were crisped, he wondered what in life he had left undone. For one thing, he had the key to Victor's Lada. It would fall apart like a wagon in the desert.

Vaksberg tipped his umbrella back to see the rain. "There is no better place for a confidential conversation than outside in the rain."

"Conversation about what?"

"You. You're the man I've been looking for. Intelligent, resourceful and with absolutely nothing to lose."

"That's a harsh assessment."

"It means you're ready for a change of fortune."

"No," Arkady said.

"Wait, you haven't even heard the offer."

"I don't want to hear the offer. Until tomorrow at least, I'm an investigator."

Dima joined them, carrying the Glock openly. He asked Vaksberg, "Is there a problem?"

"No, just a little stubbornness."

Dima asked Arkady, "What are you smiling about?"

"You're carrying a gun in a lightning storm. You're a human lightning rod."

"Go to hell." Perplexity covered the bodyguard's face.

Arkady wondered whether death would make up for a lifetime of sleep deprivation. As for hell, he suspected that it would turn out to be more like Three Stations than fiery pits of brimstone and sulfur.

Through breaks in the clouds were glimpses of blue predawn haze. The storm beat a last drumroll in retreat.

Anya got out of the car and slammed the door. She didn't look happy with anyone.

Vaksberg called, "Anya, you missed us."

She pointed to the trunk.

"This?" Dima pointed at a rope that held the trunk of the Mercedes shut.

Arkady wondered since when did Mercedes use rope to keep their trunks shut?

Dima seemed to have the same question.

As he bent for the rope the trunk popped open and a stowaway sat up in the dark of the lid. At this point bodies moved slowly. The stowaway shot Dima with muzzle flashes one, two, three. Dima tried to return fire and his infallible pistol jammed. Staggering backward, futilely squeezing a trigger that wouldn't give, he absorbed four hits before he dropped.

Slava also had a Glock. The driver's pistol didn't jam and he sprayed the Mercedes until his clip was empty, while the stowaway rolled to the side of the trunk, protected by the car's armor. Just as the idea of retreat seemed to occur to Slava, he went down.

Arkady picked up Dima's pistol. He was not a marksman— his father was an army officer who inspired in Arkady a loathing for guns—but he had grown up stripping and cleaning and generally tending them. A nine-millimeter round stood straight as a smokestack in the feed ramp of the Glock. Arkady cleared it, advanced a fresh round and, because he was a poor shot and the stowaway was hidden in the dark of the trunk, walked directly toward the car. Hurried, the figure in the trunk missed with the last rounds of his rack, strung together some "Fuck"s trying to reload a clip wrong way 'round, corrected and raised his gun when the sky split open. Facing the lightning, the stowaway blinked. The white light at his back, Arkady fired. The stowaway folded, toppled and dropped onto the ramp.

Arkady found a flashlight in the glove compartment. The shooter was a dwarf between thirty and forty years of age, muscular, in fairy-tale tights and a roll-neck sweater right out of *Snow White*, except for the Makarov nine-millimeter by his hand and a hole as round as a cigarette burn between his eyes.

"It's Dopey," Vaksberg said. "You killed Dopey."

Dima and Slava were also dead, facedown, flat as fish, blurring the water with blood. Arkady felt around the interior of the trunk and found the courtesy light taped over, pulled the tape off and discovered a plastic supermarket bag that held a change of clothes, poncho, shoes and Metro pass. No ID. Nothing worth a ride in a car trunk, let alone murder. Arkady remembered the Spartak athletic bag in the passenger compartment.

"Wait! Let me explain." Vaksberg saw Arkady veer into the car.

As Arkady unzipped the bag, credit-card receipts and dollars and euros in $10,000 rolls spilled out.

Vaksberg said, "They're donations from guests leaving the fair."

"For the Children's Fund," Anya said.

"Good luck. Once it's in militia hands, you may never see it again."

"You can explain to them," Vaksberg said. "As you said, you're still an investigator."

"Not a popular one. How much cash is in the bag?"

"A hundred thousand dollars more or less," Anya said. "The same in credit-card charges."

"Well, believe it or not, to some people that's a lot of money."

"Does the militia have to know how much money?" Vaksberg asked.

"Are you bargaining? After you almost got us killed?"

"Yes. But in my defense, you didn't seem to care one way or the other. I mean, Dopey was blasting away at you and you just walked up to him and shot him in the head."

The lightning display faded to a steady rain. The day was off to a slow start but Arkady knew that sooner or later a patrol car passing the barricade would see a limousine standing on the ramp. If they came closer they would trip over bodies. Highway police accepted bribes for almost everything. Homicide crossed the line, and when Arkady added up the bodies, he still lacked a killer of the world's most lovable dwarf.

Vaksberg asked, "What are you doing?"

Arkady put the Makarov in Vaksberg's hand, aimed at the sky and forced Vaksberg's trigger finger to squeeze off a couple of rounds.

"Making you a hero. That's to prove to a paraffin test that you fired a gun."

"You're incriminating me?"

"Not at all. I'm making you a hero. Tell them what happened just as it happened, except that I wasn't here. Act it out and get your stories straight."

Anya said, "You're leaving us?"

"That's right. The Metro will be running soon. There's a station ten minutes away. I'll find my car. It's not a Mercedes but it has no bullet holes."

Vaksberg considered his role. "So I acted in self-defense. I simply walked up to this assassin and . . . Bang!"

Arkady said nothing, although he remembered how his father put it in an army manual: *In the field, an officer should run only as a last resort and never in retreat. An officer who, under fire, can move calmly and confidently rather than race from one cover to another is worth ten brilliant tacticians.*

It was Arkady's ambition to die before he became his father.

16

Although the night's rainstorm had become morning's drizzle, Yegor insisted on getting in line for hot dogs and beer at an outdoor kiosk.

"I knew you'd come," he told Maya.

"Just until we find my baby."

The clerk in the kiosk was brown, with dark eyelids and a scholar's wire-rim glasses. He greeted Yegor tentatively. "Are you in a good mood today, my friend?"

"Definitely."

"That's good. You are always welcome when you are in a good mood."

"We've been waiting an hour for some fucking service. I'm just kidding."

"You are in a fine mood, I can see. You are our guest. Whatever you want."

"You're sure?"

"A hundred percent."

"Ali is a good guy," Yegor told Maya. "Indian or Pakistani?"

"Pakistani, please," Ali said.

"Who somehow got stuck here in Moscow."

"Stranded by fate. I came to study thirty years ago and here I am."

"Some ignorant shits gave Ali some trouble."

"Prejudice is a terrible thing. You bet I am the only Pakistani with his own kiosk."

"Prejudice." Yegor shook his head.

"But Yegor snapped his fingers and trouble disappeared. Now there are no more problems, at least not from violent youth, thanks to Yegor. You go to any other kiosk and you will hear the same story. Yegor is an important friend to have."

Yegor pushed Maya's hood back and revealed her blue scalp. "What do you think?"

"Quite exotic. How old is she?"

"Enough." Yegor collected the food and hustled Maya away, but he was pleased. "Did you hear that? You have an 'important friend.'"

"I don't want a friend, I want Katya."

"Agreed, but you can't go talking about a fucking baby with potential customers. A deal goes both ways. You have to keep your end of the bargain."

"I will."

"And stay away from Genius. He thinks you're the Virgin Mary. Don't act that way around me. You should be happy I appreciate you the way you are."

Which was nothing more than a prostitute, Maya thought. He had a way of looking at her that made her feel as if his hands crawled over her body, milking her breasts and insinuating himself between her legs, although he hadn't put a hand on her. The sensation was hypnotic and demeaning and she was sure he knew exactly what he was doing.

From hours of intimate observation she could read men. Some wanted the fantasy sex of a lifetime, worth a special chapter in a book. Some wanted to rescue an innocent girl, after sex, not before. They all wanted their money's worth.

Maya choked on her hot dog and spat it into the gutter.

"What's the matter?" Yegor asked.

"It's disgusting."

"No time to start like the present, then."

Rain slowed but didn't halt traffic and Maya wondered what passengers in the cars saw when they looked out of their cozy lives. A red stream of brake lights. A miserable few tables of CDs and DVDs under plastic. A young pimp and a whore in their element.

17

★

At three weeks Katya was still a part of her mother. Every taste and smell, warmth and touch, was her mother. When she was startled, her mother's voice soothed her, and if she could not focus farther than her mother's face, that was enough. Like the earth and moon, they seemed to be in perpetual orbits around each other, and when she woke and heard a different voice, her universe began to collapse.

The babushka Auntie Lena went into the Kazansky Station ladies' room and came out as Magdalena, still an imposing woman but colorfully dressed, with hoop earrings and hennaed hair. Basket in hand, she swept through the waiting room and joined her partner, Vadim, who had made his own transformation from drunken soldier to sober civilian. Together they left the station and crossed a side plaza with a statue of Lenin to an eight-story apartment house that overlooked Three Stations.

Usually she put on her Auntie Lena act to troll for girls. Hard class always had a couple. She would soften them up with stories about money to be made in Moscow and share snapshots of herself and a "daughter" in front of an expensive car. Why endure the boredom of a rural village giving sex for free to pimply youths when a glamorous life awaited them in exclusive clubs as escorts of the wealthiest, most dynamic men in the world? Then Vadim would step in as a menace or a friend in need; he could play it either way.

The baby was pure luck. Vadim had gotten drunk with a General Kassel, who confided how his wife was driving him crazy from wanting a baby. Not a shelter baby or some disease-ridden four-year-old delinquent, but a real baby. If possible, one with no birth certificate or history. The general was being reassigned to a new post two thousand kilometers from the old. It would be nice if they could show up without having to explain to people the miraculous addition of a newborn. The general named a figure that was astronomical. At best Magdalena and Vadim had hoped for a pregnant girl who would prefer her freedom and money in her pocket to pushing a stroller with a snotty, bawling baby. Maya was the dream candidate.

"I'll tell you just how this will go. The new parents will examine the goods—that's only natural—but they will have milk, diapers and rattle laid out so they can play mommy and daddy right away. It will take fifteen minutes. They won't want us hanging around."

At the elevator Vadim asked if the baby's diapers were clean.

"Yes. She's a beautiful baby. The general and his wife should be very happy."

"What if it's a trap?"

"You're always so nervous. That girl's not going to go to the police. She's on the run. She's our ticket. A healthy baby without a single record? Who doesn't even exist on paper? That's one in a million." When the baby started to fuss, Magdalena smiled indulgently. "Our golden baby."

The Kassels were in a second-floor apartment borrowed from friends who were on holiday. The general welcomed Vadim and Magdalena with a bonhomie that didn't hide the sweat on his forehead. He had brought in a doctor the same way a sensible man has an auto mechanic check out a used car before buying.

The general's wife bit her knuckles. Her fingertips were already raw.

She said, "You should have given me more warning."

"Everything happened so fast. And we're leaving tomorrow."

However, she was ready with nappies and formula, as Magdalena had predicted, right down to the rattle.

The doctor warned the Kassels not to get their hopes up. Generally a baby was abandoned for a reason. The chances of a street foundling not being damaged or sickly were poor.

Magdalena opened the basket. "See for yourself."

While the doctor unwrapped the swaddling Vadim tried to entertain the general and his wife with lies about the baby's provenance, how the mother was a young ballerina forced to choose between the baby and a career. He tailed off when he noticed that no one was listening. The room's attention had shifted to the examination.

The human face was a map. The shape, size and position of the ears could imply one syndrome. The spacing of eyes, mouth or nose could imply another. Or genetic damage. No alarms yet.

She was quiet while the doctor listened to her chest and back, but she fussed during her ear exam and cried vigorously about having a light shined in her eyes. The doctor looked in the baby's mouth for thrush and checked the palate. Felt her abdomen, scanned her for rashes, bruises or birthmark and finally gave her a shot of hepatitis B, which didn't make her any happier.

"This is a well-cared-for infant," the doctor said.

"Is it healthy?" the general demanded.

"Oh, yes. Off a brief examination, thriving."

"Didn't we say so?" Vadim jumped out of his seat and shook the general's hand. "Congratulations, you're a father."

"I am! I feel different already!"

"This is an expensive blue blanket. Where did you get this child?" the doctor asked, but his question was overwhelmed by the popping of champagne corks and the lusty crying of the baby.

Magdalena said, "There's a good set of lungs. That's a good sign, much better than a silent baby."

Vadim clapped. "Everyone wins. The baby gets a loving home and the mother can return with a clear conscience to the pursuit of her art."

The wife said she was afraid of holding the baby and everyone assured her it would become second nature. Magdalena and Vadim stayed for one more toast, took their money and left. The doctor left a minute later.

"We're on our own now, the three of us," Kassel said. The plan was that they would leave the next day by train to his new posting, a thousand kilometers away, in a fresh start as a happy family.

"She's rejecting the bottle," his wife said.

"She was probably breast-fed. She'll get used to the bottle."

"I can't breast-feed."

"Of course not, that's what the formula is for."

"Why did you even mention breast-feeding?"

"It's no big thing."

"It is a big thing. She wants her mother."

"She's just hungry. As soon as she adjusts to the bottle, she will be fine."

"She doesn't like me."

"You're new to her."

"Look at her." The baby was red from kicking and squalling. "She hates me."

"You have to hold her."

"You hold her. Why did you bring her? Why is she here?"

"Because every time we see a baby, you tell me how much you want one."

"My baby, not somebody else's."

"You said you wanted to adopt."

"Some idiot from a shelter?"

"This is a perfect baby."

"If it were a perfect baby, it would shut up."

"Do you know how much I paid for this baby?"

"You paid for a baby? That's like paying for a cat."

And the baby cried.

There were no complaints because everyone in the surrounding apartments was at work. The baby cried itself to exhaustion, slept and regained enough strength to cry again. Just in case, the general turned on a television with the volume up. His wife pulled on a sleep mask and went to bed. Neither tried to feed the baby again.

During a lull in the crying, he carried a pillowcase stuffed with baby paraphernalia to a refuse bin in the basement. When he returned he found the baby on the floor, hoarse from crying, and his wife standing over it with her fists against her ears.

He asked, "What are you doing?"

"I can't sleep."

"So you moved her?"

"Someone has to. It just keeps crying. You're a general; order it to shut up."

"I'll get rid of it."

"Then do it."

In the bedroom closet Kassel found a shoe box complete with tissue to nestle in. As if that were an amenity.

The baby was a mess, its eyes swollen almost shut, nose stopped with mucus. A wheezing, shivering, smaller baby. He put it in the shoe box and taped the lid shut. Decided on no airholes. Put the shoe box in an oversize shopping bag and took the stairs down rather than meet anyone in the elevator.

The general didn't know Moscow well but his plan was to leave the bag amid the crowds and confusion of Three Stations. The problem was that when he got to Kazansky Station, he discovered how little confusion there actually was. Everyone moved with a purpose and had four or five eyes instead of two and all on the watch for suspicious behavior. He regretted the shopping bag; unfurled, it was large and gaudy and had an Italian logo that drew attention. He had to be casual. Unrattled. Even so, when the box shifted in the bag he panicked and headed for the nearest tunnel. He found himself in a pedestrian underpass that was a gallery of stalls staffed with women who would no doubt detect a baby's least whimper. Kassel was grateful to reach the blaring speakers of a music stall.

The problem was that his wife was so high-strung. She wasn't meant for the army life of moving from one dreary outpost to another, living in cold-water housing and forced to be grateful for that at a time when thousands of officers of the highest ranks were being shoved into early retirement. She said a million times that the only thing that would make her happy was a child.

Toward the end of the stalls, militia officers were stopping people at random to check their papers and search their bags. It was a fishing expedition for bribes and Kassel's impulse was to backtrack because he had forgotten his ID. If he had been in uniform, he would have been waved through. Instead the flow of foot traffic trapped him and pushed him toward an officer who was already reaching for the bag when a gang of street kids, none older than eight, squirmed through. They came and went like a swarm of gnats and collapsed the line, and by the time order was restored, the general was safe on the other side.

Now that he believed that luck was on his side, he marched directly to the boarding platforms, where he joined a crowd of passengers. He set the shopping bag down and stared down the track with a cigarette between his teeth, the picture of impatience, moving only to avoid the giant suitcases of day peddlers and the sharp edge of porters' carts. The baby was silent. No kicking, no fuss. Although the general took no pleasure in harming a baby in any way, he felt he had kept damage to a minimum.

Simple plans were the best, the general thought. When the train pulled in, he would join the disembarking riders and leave the shopping bag and baby behind. At this point it seemed providential that he hadn't had an ID to show the militia. There was no way to identify him. It was as if the baby had passed through the world as undetected as a gamma ray. As if it had never existed at all, not officially.

People stirred as a commuter train approached across a field of rails. This was the end of the line. As it drew closer the general saw riders standing in the aisles, folding their newspapers, closing their cell phones. He was in the perfect position to slip among them.

Only where was the Italian bag?

The bag had been at his feet and he hadn't strayed more than a few steps, yet it had disappeared. In the press of riders leaving the train and others boarding, the bag had vanished.

He melded with the stream of arrivals. Either the bag had been kicked into the gap between the platform and the train or a thief had unwittingly done him a favor. The general felt a guilty relief and could barely keep from running.

The scare came later, in the middle of the night, when two detectives knocked on the apartment door. Kassel felt that someone at the platform must have seen him with the bag. But the detectives only asked questions about a dead prostitute in a totally unrelated case and he honestly said he couldn't help. So, overall, he felt he had done fairly well. In fact, the memory of the baby was already starting to fade.

At sunrise a half-dozen runaway kids hit a twenty-four-hour supermarket on the same street as police headquarters. They came like a gang of mice and created as much nuisance as possible, stuffing jars of Spanish olives and tins of tuna fish into their pockets, picking over organic fruit and avocados with their dirty hands. Some days ice cream was the target, other days any aerosol to sniff.

Security cameras tried to follow them, although grown men and women chasing homeless six-year-olds did not make a pretty picture. The staff ejected the kids as discreetly as possible and took a quick inventory of stolen items, petty stuff not worth reporting to the police, including sliced bread, strawberry jam, orangeade, energy bars, baby formula, nappies and a bottle.

18

Things were never what they seemed. Maya had the face of an angel, but when Zhenya opened his eyes, she was gone and with her his money.

He searched the casino, the bank and security rooms, the restrooms and dealers' lounge. Whispering her name, he searched among the slots, the one-armed guards of the Kremlin, as if they were carrying her off to a tower and some jolly bacchanal. There were no signs of resistance, not a stack of chips toppled, not a single plastic pearl spilled from the crown jewels. He tried to sleep but his anger was a match struck before a mirror and he saw what a fool he had been.

Bitch!

She had turned him from a hustler into an easy mark. It wasn't as if there was anything romantic or sexual between him and Maya. Zhenya wouldn't have presumed. But he thought they had a good relationship. He brought Moscow know-how and intellect, while Maya contributed physical daring, sexual experience and, by virtue of being a mother, adulthood. Assuming that her name really was Maya or there really was a baby or that anything she said was true. Where was she now? In his mind's eye he saw Maya and Yegor on a bed of twisted sheets. When he imagined Yegor's grunts and her submissive whimper, Zhenya covered his ears. Or perhaps Yegor wanted to show Maya who was boss and was giving her a rough ride over the fender of a car. Zhenya had never appreciated how masochistic his imagination was. It was like setting a house on fire and choosing to sit in the flames.

There was a more practical problem. If Maya switched sides, she was sure to tell Yegor about the Peter the Great. The casino's stock of liquor alone was worth thousands. Yegor would rip out what he could carry and trash what he couldn't, which was a shame because there was a certain perfection about a casino. The brushed felt of the tables. The chips neatly stacked by color. The new dice. The sealed decks of cards.

He spent the day waiting for night, watching the clouds grow thick and dark, and he remembered how once when he was four years old he and the other kids in the shelter were taken to a petting zoo. The only animal Zhenya was interested in petting was the sheep, because their fleece was always described in children's books as so soft and white. Instead their fleece turned out to be gray and greasy and knotted with shit. For a long time he thought that was what clouds were like.

In the daytime Yegor might be anywhere but in the evening he could reliably be found around Lubyanka Square. One entire side of the square was taken up by the Lubyanka itself, a handsome eight-story building of yellow brick with a subtle illumination like votive candles. There was a time when vans arrived at the Lubyanka every night with a haul of bewildered professors, doctors, poets, even party members accused of being foreign agents, wreckers, saboteurs.

Now no one lingered in front of the Lubyanka, any more than they would walk under a ladder or let a black cat cross their path. Not that anything could happen, but why wake the devil?

Directly across the square was a toy store, the biggest in Russia, with an indoor carousel that turned under chandeliers fit for a palace. Now the store was dark and gutted, ready for renovation and efficiency. Whimsy was the first item to go.

Children still came. They vamped in doorways, bummed cigarettes, trotted beside slow-moving cars. At eleven years of age, some of the boys already had the heavy gaze and sullen slouch of rough trade.

Zhenya looked straight ahead rather than meet the predatory gazes of drivers cruising by. Lubyanka Square was not top browsing for pedophiles—that honor went to Three Stations and the streets around the Bolshoi—but it was a fair start for a pimp as young as Yegor.

Zhenya was determined not to let Maya walk all over him. Yegor would interpret that as weakness and an invitation to double the price of "protection." Zhenya wasn't going to wait. He knew from chess that the player who moved first had an advantage.

Nevertheless, he shied away when a Volvo station wagon came to a stop and the man on the passenger side called him over to the curb.

Zhenya said, "I'm not . . ."

"Not what?" The voice was flat.

"For . . . you know."

"Know what?" The man's face was a gray shadow. The same with the driver, as if they had been shaped from the same clay. Their station wagon bore dents and creases of rust, suggesting that the vehicle had been rolled, left for dead and resurrected.

"I don't know," Zhenya said.

The man said, "We're looking for a girl. She ran away from home and her mother and father are very worried about her. There's a reward for helping us."

He showed Zhenya a photocopy of Maya sitting with the baby in the bus shelter. The baby existed and Maya smiled as if she could hold it forever. Zhenya made much of trying to see the picture in better light.

"It's her baby?"

"Yeah. That's another reason to find her. Her parents are worried sick about the baby."

"Who are you?"

"Not that it matters, but we're her uncles. It's family business."

"What's her name?"

"Maya. Maya Ivanova Pospelova. The person who delivers her gets a reward of a hundred dollars. The last time anybody saw her she dyed her hair red. Keep the picture. There are two cell-phone numbers on the other side."

"She's pretty."

The driver said, "She's a whore."

The car moved on to a streetlamp at the end of the block where a convertible with the top down had attracted a circle of boys. The station wagon rolled to a stop and flashed its high beams. The convertible was a BMW, a German driving machine unlikely to make room for a wreck, and its driver made a rude gesture without bothering to turn and look behind. When the Volvo rolled forward and tapped the rear bumper of the BMW, its driver called on the heavens to rain shit on idiots who drove shit cars. The passenger emerged from the Volvo, opened its tailgate and drew out a long-handled shovel. He marched to the front of the convertible and brought the shovel edge down on the hood. The driver of the BMW ducked so quickly he broke his nose on the steering wheel and blood covered his mouth and chin. That was only teeing up. The second swing had sufficient whip to buckle the hood and a third set off the windshield wipers. Three swings were enough. The convertible rode over the curb in its haste to escape and the Volvo took its place at the curb. The boys had retreated but in a minute they crowded the car for pictures of Maya.

Zhenya had no idea where Maya and Yegor were. All he could do was race up one block and down the next, avoid being hit by the high-speed traffic exiting the roundabout and dart between the cars slowly cruising the side streets. He wasn't used to running and he blamed Arkady as a poor role model. The second time around, the blocks were longer, the air thinner. He was staggering to a stop when he became aware that the Volvo station wagon, its lights out, was immediately behind him. It didn't matter; he couldn't take another step.

The man on the passenger side got out and opened a rear door for Zhenya. He gave the boy a chance to catch his breath.

"Where is she?"

Zhenya had not panicked in a thousand games of chess, which only underlined the difference between fantasy and reality. A multitude of escape scenarios always came to mind over a chessboard but the man had a grip on Zhenya's arm that squeezed his bicep in two.

"I don't know anything."

"Then you have nothing to worry about."

He was pushing Zhenya into the backseat when an older boy skidded up to the Volvo and said they had the wrong guy; the girl they wanted was with a pimp named Yegor only a few blocks away.

To the men Zhenya no longer existed and he found himself sitting on the curb loathing his newfound cowardice.

19

★

Arkady slept a luxurious two hours and would have stayed in bed longer but for a muffled sound at the front door.

The apartment originally had fireplaces. They were bricked in and unusable, but the hardware remained and Arkady chose a poker. Wearing only pajama bottoms, he whipped the door open and found one of the up-and-coming young men from the prosecutor's staff on his knees with a letter he had been trying to slip under the door. The up-and-comer saw the poker, jumped to his feet and rushed down the stairs.

The letter was handwritten, which showed Zurin cared. It was also typical that the prosecutor would have enlisted someone else to deliver it, one of the lads who regarded Arkady as ancient and as unpredictable as a loaded harquebus.

Suspended for cause . . . poor judgment . . . calling into question and undermining the aims . . . concocting cases . . . flouting the chain of command . . . given every chance . . . forced to take action . . . deepest regrets . . . your firearm and identification.

Zurin's signature was twice as firm and twice as large as usual.

Arkady turned on the television. Sasha Vaksberg led the newscasts. How could he not? A famous billionaire kills a would-be assassin? And not just any assassin but one disguised as Dopey? A police spokesman solemnly pointed to bullet dents on the limousine's trunk and fender. Unfortunately for the viewers, rain had washed away the blood.

He turned the set off. This was the sort of case that Petrovka felt two ways about. Three dead bodies drove up the crime rate. On the other hand, they also drove up the solution rate, which had been lagging badly. There was a niggling question of why Vaksberg's driver had ignored construction barriers to park on an unfinished highway ramp. The man was dead and it didn't matter. Keep it simple.

Zurin's letter, however, had also accused Arkady of "concocting cases." Translated, that meant the prosecutor was closing the investigation of the body found at Three Stations. Forget the obscene pose and the ether in her lungs. Her body had been reduced to ashes and all that was left of Vera Antonova was a death certificate that was moved from a file labeled *Open* to a file labeled *Closed*.

So it was over. Arkady rang Victor to call off the rendezvous at Three Stations, but Victor's mobile phone was off. He tried calling Zhenya. Zhenya didn't answer, and Arkady discovered that the number he had for Eva was no longer in service, meaning the last link of communication he had with her was gone. Or, more likely, that their connection had died long ago and he had been talking to echoes.

With the curtains closed, the apartment was a sensory deprivation tank. Once upon a time such a weepy day would have invited self-pity and thoughts of suicide. But his heart wasn't in it anymore. The blackness of mood, the single-mindedness that was demanded for self-destruction was missing. The boy in the morgue who drained himself as white as alabaster had displayed the proper sense of commitment. He deserved more than his mother's dismissive "Burn him." Arkady expected that in his own case, if he did blow his head off, it would please Zurin far too much.

There was a rap on the door. Arkady assumed that the investigator who delivered the letter had found the courage to return for Arkady's official ID. However, when he opened the door, he was hit in the chest by an empty red-and-white athletic bag. Anya Rudikova marched in. She was in the same black outfit as the night before, only now it clung like wet crepe.

"You smug bastard."

"What are you talking about?" Arkady pulled on a T-shirt.

"What do you think is in the bag?"

"When I looked, money."

"How much?"

"That's not my business."

"There was over a hundred thousand dollars in cash. Now there's none. The militia got it all because you wouldn't help. They say they have to ascertain the ownership of the money. They won't accept our receipts. All you had to do was take the bag with you. You didn't. You owe me a hundred thousand dollars."

"Get it from Sasha. He's the billionaire."

"He didn't leave the money. You did."

It dawned on Arkady that Anya was in wet clothes and probably had had no sleep at all. If he was exhausted, so was she.

"We'll talk tomorrow," he said.

There was a problem. The militia had taken the key to her apartment to search it for other athletic bags stuffed with cash; if she had one, why not more? And they confiscated the key in case they wanted to return and search the flat again.

"I'm locked out," Anya admitted.

It was an opportunity for Arkady to be smug, but he let it pass.

They were adults. To get into a friend's apartment would have taken Anya an hour at least. Even if Arkady's flat was the last place on earth she wanted to be, logic and a bout of violent shivering made it the only choice.

"Please," he said.

After a brief show of resistance, she hurried to the bathroom and shut the door behind her. He sat dumbfounded by the situation. A man and a woman find themselves in an apartment against their will. Why should there be a sexual context? There wouldn't be if he were dealing with a male colleague. It was a pro forma fantasy. But when she showered he not only heard her, he could feel the hot pinpricks of water move down her neck, her back, her stomach. He had a glass of vodka and a cigarette.

Through the door he offered her clothes that Eva had left in a suitcase under the bed. Instead she emerged in a shirt of his with the sleeves rolled up.

"It's bad enough I'm here, I'm not going to wear another woman's clothes."

The shirt hung to her knees. He couldn't think of any compliment that covered the situation.

She said, "Anyway, I just need to close my eyes."

"Take the bed. I'll take the sofa in the living room." It wasn't much of a sofa and it wasn't much of a living room. He had taken down all the posters and photos that he and Eva had chosen together. The sofa was little larger than a sled.

"I'm not going to kick you out of your own bed."

"It's called hospitality," Arkady said.

"I am not your guest. I'll take the sofa." She sat on it with an air of fait accompli. "It's nearer the front door and you won't even hear me when I leave."

He gave up. She was impossible. Before she arrived at his doorstep, he had considered the possibility of sleep. Now his eyes were wide-open.

She said from the sofa, "Dopey never had a chance."

Talking to Anya was like skydiving, Arkady thought. You were at terminal velocity before you knew it.

She said, "That was why you could walk right up to him. You had the advantage."

"What advantage?"

"You didn't care if you died. For you it was a win-win situation."

"The only advantage is that when a lot of shots are fired, the trigger gets heavy and the kick gets high."

"Not you. You shot him right between the eyes."

"And saved your life."

"Killed Dopey and gained control of the scene. You knew the militia would confiscate the bag."

"At the time, the bag was a minor issue."

"Not to me. Was there something dirty about the bag? You thought it was drug money, didn't you?"

"I had no idea one way or the other."

"But with fashion people there are a lot of drugs."

"With police too."

"You're so fair-minded."

"I'm trying." Arkady didn't know how she had turned the conversation around, but she had.

"So it could be drug money?"

"Who knows?"

"And I could be a whore."

"I never said that."

"Some whore who writes about other whores who wear

the latest fashions. Fuck her, you say. Let her be robbed. Keep
her busy all night answering the same questions over and over
while the bag gets lighter and lighter. I hear that you're cozy
with Prosecutor Zurin."

"Like brothers."

"Do you share your cut with him?"

Arkady swung out of bed. Anya tried to see him as he disappeared in the living room and reappeared in the kitchen. She
watched him approach with something white and she flinched
as he thrust it at her.

"What is it?"

"A letter from my friend Prosecutor Zurin. There's a lamp
on the end table. Feel free to search the apartment. If you find
a hundred thousand dollars, it's yours."

He didn't wait to see if she read it.

Arkady woke briefly. In the darkness he became aware of another person not just nearby but radiating warmth. The scent of
her was all-enveloping and he was so aroused it hurt. He could
tell by her shifting on the sofa that Anya was also awake and
anticipation and frustration hung in the air in equal amounts
until he brushed them aside as products of his imagination.

When Arkady woke again, at noon, and spread the drapes,
Anya was gone. On the pavement umbrellas were open. At his
end of the street the pothole was expanding. A battery of workers, all women, shoveled hot asphalt down its maw. He watched
a rubber boot go under.

Banners for the Nijinsky Fair sagged like shrouds. Arkady
wondered what luxury or sensation was left. A diamond-studded
elephant? Human sacrifice? Or would Sasha Vaksberg himself be
an added attraction as a defender of the moneyed class? Arkady
admitted to himself that he had assumed Vaksberg would protect
Anya and that assumption was proving to be wrong. Smug, in fact.

★

Arkady phoned Willi, who said he couldn't talk. "We've got two boys who crashed on the Ring Road, a sniffer, an indigent pneumonia, a fall from a height, a slashed neck and now this threesome of gunshot victims and they've pressed me back into service."

Arkady asked, "Is one of the three a dwarf?"

Willi took his time answering. Arkady heard the snap of a rib cutter in the background.

"A remarkable guess."

"Tell me about him."

"It's no less work. People think, oh, a dwarf should be fast. Nothing could be further from the truth. There are different types of dwarfs and unusual factors."

"I thought he was shot."

"Yes."

"Isn't that the main factor?"

"Don't get smart. I'm not even supposed to talk to you."

"Who told you that?"

"The director. And Prosecutor Zurin. Zurin said that he was going to dismiss you. Did he?"

"Not yet," Arkady said.

This had to be done delicately. He had no authority. It was like casting a small lure on a lightweight line to a dimple in the water where there might be fish.

"What do you mean?" Willi asked.

"I mean that ordering someone to alter an autopsy report is serious business. You have the power—"

Willi hung up.

Well, that was feeble, Arkady thought. He had used psychology when he should have used blackmail.

His cell phone vibrated. Willi was back.

"Sorry, I had to get a cigarette."

"Take your time."

"This is what happened. Zurin and the director had me cut the girl's lung again. By then the smell of ether had dissipated. They said if I couldn't replicate my findings, the autopsy report had to be revised."

"Couldn't you detect it by other means?"

"Not after they're cremated."

"Already?"

"It was the wish of the family."

"Where's the dwarf?" Arkady asked.

"Here under a sheet. We're waiting for a table."

"Has he been identified?"

"No. We know nothing about him."

"Lift the sheet."

"Oh. Okay," said Willi. "We know something now. He's blue with tattoos from head to toe. He's a con."

Prison tattoos were done with a sharp hook and "ink" made out of urine and soot. Once under the skin, the pigment was blue and slightly blurred, but behind bars, tattoos were more than art; they were autobiography. For anyone who could read the symbols, a tattooed man was an open book.

Arkady said, "Tell me what you see."

"All kinds. Madonna and Child, teardrops, cats, spiderweb, Iron Cross, bloody dagger, barbed wire. The works."

"As soon as we hang up, I want you to take pictures of Dopey's tattoos with your cell phone and send them to me. I have an expert."

20

Itsy's original family was an addicted mother and abusive father. Their house had been like a listing ship, filthy clothes and
empty bottles rolled to one side, bills underfoot and electricity
cut off half the time.

The old man raised guard dogs for security agencies. Alsa-
tians. Rottweilers. Money in that, but it went down her father's
throat. Any money that made it home was an oversight. He
smelled like the dogs. Man's best friend. Loyal.

By the time Itsy was twelve, her older brothers had run
off. Lost out on the family business, a thriving enterprise that
would have gone to them if, God forbid, anything happened to
their father. Good real estate too, if Moscow spread in his direction. So he informed anyone trapped between him and a wall.

Times Itsy missed school were when she had no shoes. It didn't
bother her father or mother that she didn't know much more than
the alphabet and numbers, and when the school sent people to
check on her well-being, she hid rather than be seen in rags.

Her job from the age of six was to clean the pens and dog run. Her father fed them. His credo was that "Him what feeds 'em is their muvver." And then he would stagger out in a suit of plastic armor and train them to attack.

With no companions and little else to do, Itsy spent hours with the dogs, playing with them or simply lying with them in a heap. Each dog had his own personality. The dogs were supposed to be kept apart in their own pens, but Itsy let them mix. Their eyes followed everything she did.

One winter evening her father came home early, drunk and bruised, the sullen loser of a street fight, when he found the dogs milling freely around Itsy. The dogs read his mood and drew closer to her.

"Growl at me?" He pulled out his trouser belt and bawled, "Out of the way!"

He might have cowed the pack and gained control if Itsy had not been present, if the first swing of the belt had not drawn a stripe of blood across her cheek.

One moment he was up and the next he was just a pair of legs kicking at the bottom of a frenzy that Itsy could not have stopped if she tried.

After, when the dogs tired of dragging her father's body back and forth, she put each in its pen, washed and dried the bloody money she found in her father's pocket and put on as many clothes as possible. He was too heavy to move, and the ground too hard to dig a grave, however shallow.

Her mother had slept through it all. Itsy would have left a note if she knew how to write. She would have written, "Please Feed the Dogs."

Petra had stopped her cart at Aisle 3—Coffee & Tea, apparently undecided between bags of Sumatran or Colombian, whole bean or ground. She was nine years old and had the straight hair and broad face of a Romanian princess. She put the Colombian back on the shelf and picked up a French roast.

Strolling on Aisle 5—Biscuits & Cookies, a cigarette cocked by his ear, Leo couldn't help but look like imminent trouble. He carried a "maybe"; a "maybe" was a mesh bag that everyone used to carry in case they saw anything for sale. Leo had long legs and loved to run. He was eleven.

Lisa was in Frozen Foods. She had bow lips, blue eyes, a halo of golden hair and a blank expression. Her best friend, Milka, was in Produce comparing cantaloupes, giving each the sniff test, the knock test, the squeeze. Milka was as plain as Lisa was beautiful, but she wore braces on her teeth, a sign of relative affluence. The girls were ten.

The supermarket was part of a French chain and there was a special emphasis on dishes with Gallic style like pâté, cheeses and duck à l'orange ready for the microwave. Rabbits fluffy and skinned hung in a meat department designed to look like a true *boucherie*. A café served crêpes and *croque-monsieur*.

Behind a one-way mirror over the lamb chops the floor manager flipped through a face book until he found a match with Lisa. Uniformed security guards were stationed at the entrance and emergency exits, wine department and caviar bar. When the chief counted four runaways, he went out on the floor. Although none of the kids had as yet done anything illegal, he wanted them to know he was keeping an eye on them, so he was looking the wrong way when the automatic door opened and a black Alsatian police dog on a loose leash bounded down Aisle 1—Breads & Baked Goods, followed by a girl.

The dog had a deep bark and the impact of a cannonball. In Produce he brushed a table and spilled lemons across the floor. Cans of stewed tomatoes rolled in his wake. A security man attempting to block Aisle 7—Pet Food grasped air as the dog leaped into the meat bin and came out with a filet mignon hanging from his jaws. Two guards who tried to corner the dog between Ice Cream and Frozen Foods were left in a tangle of overturned carts.

For the dog, it was a game. It crouched like a sprinter, barked and allowed the guards to get only so near before it made a feint in one direction and took off in another. When the floor manager approached with a can of pepper spray, the dog instantly retreated. Meanwhile regular customers abandoned their carts and made an exodus to the street. All the runaways vanished and, suddenly, so did the dog.

What confused the floor manager was that after a physical count and an inventory of receipts, nothing had been taken from the floor except the steak. It was hard to bring charges against a dog. A day later, however, the stockroom manager noticed what else was missing.

While his staff had watched the antics taking place on the other side of the one-way mirror, someone had walked in the backdoor of the stockroom and left with six cases of dry baby formula, four jumbo bags of disposable diapers and two cartons of premixed formula in bottles for babies on the move.

Itsy said, "She likes the bottle."

"I'd rather breast-feed. Yum yum."

"Shut up."

"What a dirty mind."

"Boys are disgusting."

Leo said, "That was so great when Tito smashed into the lemons."

"Tito's a good dog."

"Tito's the best."

The dog raised his massive head at the sound of his name and cast a loving gaze toward Itsy.

Emma, the youngest, looked like a rag doll. She was the most fascinated. "Did she cry much?"

"Not a lot."

"We should send Tito back for more steaks."

"They never saw us," Peter said.

Klim said, "We could have gone back to the storeroom and taken twice as much. We could have cleaned them out." With their pallor he and Peter looked like junior convicts. Klim was nine and Peter was ten.

"I changed the baby three times. She was kind of runny," Itsy said.

"She looks tired. Did she sleep?"

"She fussed."

"Is this her name, Itsy?" Emma held up an embroidered corner of the blanket.

"Read it yourself." There was a polite silence because everyone knew Itsy couldn't read.

"Katya," Emma said in a small voice.

"Can we turn on the radio?"

"Keep it low."

"How long can we stay here?"

"We'll see."

The situation seemed ideal: a workers' trailer that had suddenly appeared in an unused repair shed in the yard of Kazansky Station. The trailer had bunks, however stained and filthy, and a potbellied stove. The trailer wasn't going anywhere. Its tires had been flat; now they were shredded.

The shed itself was a steel hangar open at one end to the station's yard. Rails led to trenches deep enough for a man to stand in for undercarriage repair. Or had at one time. Waist-high grass suggested a long spell of inactivity.

"It's spooky."

"Tito will let us know if anyone comes."

Lisa asked, "What if Yegor comes?"

Milka opened a knife. "If he comes anywhere near you again, I'll cut his balls off."

Itsy had no such illusions. She preferred to stay one step ahead of Yegor. Yegor was a grown-up by comparison with anyone in her crew.

"Why would they want a trailer in a train shed?"

"I don't know, but they did and we're going to use it. We can take care of ourselves. And we have Tito. And now we have a baby and that makes us a family."

21

★

Victor expounded on tattoos in the café at Yaroslavl Station. He touched the screen on Arkady's phone and enlarged the picture as he went.

"Think of a criminal's tattoos as a painting by the School of Rubens, a painting done by different hands at different times, with sections or faces added or obscured, some areas left blank in anticipation of notable events or cramped by bad planning.

"Let's begin with the Madonna and Child. This domestic scene tells us that Dopey was not born to a family of the bourgeoisie but to a family of honest criminals. The tattooing is primitive, although the faces were retouched later. The cat tattoos celebrate an early career as a burglar, and you can imagine from the spryness of these cats how a dwarf can get into all sorts of spaces.

"As he gets older and heavier, he graduates to murder. Three tears for three victims, as if he gave a fuck. He's been imprisoned four times. The barbs on barbed wire tell you how many years. The spiderweb on his shoulder means he's addicted, probably to heroin, because there is a surreal quality to the web reminiscent of Dalí."

There was a new vigor to Victor, Arkady thought. For a man who should be struggling with the DTs, he looked surprisingly hale.

"You can trust a criminal's hide more than a banker's business card. The card says he has offices in Moscow, London and Hong Kong even though he's never been further than Minsk. But when a convict wears a tattoo for a crime he hasn't honestly committed, other cons will tattoo 'Liar' right across his face."

"It's good to know there is integrity somewhere in the world."

"The old cachet isn't there. Now every housewife has a tattoo on her ass. Nobody behind bars is satisfied with homemade ink when their girlfriends are trotting around on the outside with their pants half off and a tat that glows in the dark." He broke off to ask, "Worried?"

"They have to send me a letter of suspension and a letter of dismissal. Zurin only sent one."

"You're sure? Anyway, I can't believe that I'm with the man who killed Dopey the Dwarf. Does a curse come with that?"

"Probably," Arkady agreed.

"Don't worry about it. You are so fucked a curse would be superfluous."

Victor ducked out before the bill came. Arkady asked the waiter if he had ever noticed a boy hustle chess in the station.

The waiter leaned in thought.

"A thin boy?"

"Yes. Named Zhenya."

"I don't know about any Zhenya. This one's called 'Genius.'"

"That's close enough."

"He's in and out of the station all the time."

"Has he been in today?"

"No. He might be taking a day off. He had a big bust-up with his girlfriend last night. Right here."

Arkady wasn't sure he heard right. "A girlfriend?"

"A beauty queen."

"He has a beautiful girlfriend?"

"With a shaved head."

"With a shaved head, no less?" The Zhenya that Arkady knew did not hang out with such a trendy crowd. In fact, he hung out with no one at all. "I think we're talking about two different people."

The waiter shrugged.

"A shame. She was special but, like I say, a bitch."

22

Four men gathered at a round table: Senior Investigator Renko, District Prosecutor Zurin, Assistant Deputy Prosecutor General Gendler and a ministry elder called Father Iosif, who was as silent and motionless as a stuffed owl. He had long since passed the mandatory retirement age of sixty and, presumably, rolled on with year-to-year contracts. No one knew exactly what Father Iosif's status was. No one ever heard him speak.

Zurin had never looked better; fit and eager for the fray. Under Yeltsin, he had been round and apoplectic; in Putin's regime, Zurin ate sensibly, exercised and lost weight. A stack of dossiers tied with self-important red ribbons stood by him.

Gendler had placed Arkady's ID and pistol, a nine-millimeter Makarov, in the middle of the table and noted what an ideal setting for Russian roulette it was.

"Except, you need a revolver," Arkady said. "A cylinder to spin. Otherwise you've pretty much eliminated the element of chance."

"Who needs chance?" Gendler placed a tape recorder on the table. He pressed Record and identified site, date, time and persons present for a hearing on dismissal.

It took Arkady a moment to realize what was transpiring. "Wait, this is a hearing on suspension."

"No, this is a hearing on dismissal."

"I received the letter for suspension late last night. I have it." He passed the letter to the assistant deputy, who laid it aside without reading it.

"Duly noted, a typographical error. However, this is the second hearing. For whatever reason, you did not attend the first."

"I'd like to change the date."

"Out of the question. The panel is assembled. We have a quorum and we have the supporting dossiers and material that Prosecutor Zurin has brought. We can't ask him to cart those back and forth at your convenience."

"I need time to prepare materials."

"It's your second letter. The first letter went out a month ago. Your time for preparation ran out yesterday."

"I received no first letter."

"I received mine," said Zurin.

"Then I would have been suspended."

"You were."

Which explained the lack of caseload coming from the prosecutor. Nothing could hide the triumph in Zurin's face. He had played his part perfectly and so, in his ignorance, had Arkady.

"I was in the office every day."

"Preparing for this dismissal hearing, I assumed," Zurin said. "I didn't get in your way."

Gendler said, "Renko, you brought nothing else to substantiate your defense?"

"No."

"But you have been active. According to Prosecutor Zurin,

two nights ago you were seen leaving a sobriety station. Yesterday you altered autopsy reports in an effort to fake a murder."

"The autopsy was not faked. I was assisting on a murder case. We may have a serial killer."

"Today you claim to have discovered a serial killer. Every detective's wet dream. I'm sorry, but in a contest of claim and counterclaim, I have to go with hard evidence, and you don't have any."

Arkady said, "I suggest that we go over the prosecutor's evidence to see how hard it really is."

"We don't have time. We're overwhelmed. So, do you expect to contest your dismissal or not? I should warn you—"

"No."

"You are not contesting your dismissal?"

"I am not."

"He's folding," Gendler told Zurin, half in surprise.

"I heard. So he won't be needing these." Zurin gathered Arkady's ID and gun from the table.

"Not the gun." Arkady clamped Zurin's wrist.

"It's property of the state."

"Please, gentlemen." The assistant deputy tried to separate them.

Arkady bent Zurin's fingers back. The prosecutor let go and said, "See, he's crazy. He attacked me right in front of witnesses."

"Read it." Arkady passed the gun to Gendler.

"Read what?"

"On the slide."

The engraving on the gun was as fine as calligraphy.

"'This firearm and a lifetime license are awarded to Honored Investigator A. K. Renko in gratitude from the Russian people.'"

"It's mine," Arkady said.

"I'll take that under consideration." Gendler kept the pistol.

"Renko," Father Iosif said. "Now there was a son of a bitch."

Everyone froze. Gendler was dumbfounded. No one had ever heard Father Iosif utter a word before.

"He keeps the gun," Father Iosif said, and the decision was made.

Each desk in the squad room was a stage with a different drama. A murderer handcuffed to his chair. A profusely sweating tourist who kept feeling his pockets in case his passport materialized. An old lady whose cat was missing. She had brought pictures. Besides mug shots of professional criminals, a bulletin board carried photos of soldiers gone AWOL, a new handful every day. A goldfish nibbled on a companion.

Arkady arrived with a bag of cold sodas. Day three was the day the snakes of alcohol usually came out, but Victor was bright as a robin.

"You got here without incident? You didn't roll the car? None of the doors blew off?"

"It's in mint condition."

"How did the meeting go?"

"It was for dismissal, not suspension."

Victor sat up. "You're not serious."

"They seemed to be. They have no sense of humor."

"You're out?"

"A mere citizen."

"That's as 'mere' as it gets. Do you want me to kill Zurin? I will. I'd be happy to."

"No, but I appreciate the offer."

"You can't win in this fucking world. Let's get drunk tonight. Let's get drunk until our eyes swim. What do you say?"

Arkady sat at Victor's computer. On its screen a beautiful model with voluminous blond hair and Nordic-blue eyes was wrapped in a wolf jacket and matching cap. In the background the onion domes of St. Basil's glowed in golden sunlight.

"You're making progress," Arkady said.

"Suspended, dismissed, you don't let go."

"Not yet."

A label on the photograph said, *Oksana Petrovna is represented by Venus International.*

At the tap of a key the scene changed to a studio apartment. Oksana Petrovna lay on her back in the middle of the floor with her head resting in a pool of blood, hands on her hips. Her leather trousers and underpants were pulled down to her ankles. Possibly the first position of ballet. Hard to say. The date of the photo was two years ago. According to the notes, a homeless man confessed and then recanted.

Arkady said, "It looks like she was hit from behind."

"Yeah, then they beat some poor bastard until he would confess to buggering the czar. After that, the case went cold."

Arkady punched up the next screen. Inna Ustinova looked younger than her thirty-two years. A yoga instructor, she had been married twice, once to an American who had promised her Malibu, California, and delivered Columbus, Ohio. According to her entry in Facebook, she had resolved to date only Russians. Her ambition? To dance at the Club Nijinsky. Her body was discovered six months before in a culvert at a dog show in Ismailova Park. She was naked from the waist down, with no signs of violence, an apparent overdose. Her feet were apart and her arms stretched like wings, as in the second position.

"That's it?" Arkady asked.

"That's it."

"No third position?"

"Yeah. It's called pissing into the wind."

"Venus International. Is that a well-known modeling agency?"

"I called a friend. She says it's so-so."

"The name is not quite right," Arkady said.

"What do you mean?"

"Well, it's not quite right, is it? 'Venus' suggests a little more."

"You mean . . ."

"Exactly."

"More . . ."

"Yes."

"Well, they used to present what they called 'private modeling' of lingerie and the like but they've been on the up-and-up for years."

"Was Venus at any time also a matchmaking agency? Beautiful Russian brides for lonely American men?"

"When Venus started out, it tried to be any number of things. I know what you're after. Did the paths of these two women ever cross?"

"Did they?"

"Ustinova was in Facebook. She had a million 'friends' but Oksana Petrovna was not one of them. These women lived in Moscow but in two different worlds."

"Did they club?"

"Yes. A pretty girl can always get in a club. Models like Ustinova are regulars at the Nijinsky and at a dozen other clubs. Now, if Petrovna had been a Nijinsky dancer like Vera, there might be a tidy little connection, only she wasn't. So that's that."

"Did she try?"

"What do you mean?"

"Did Petrovna audition to be a dancer at the Club Nijinsky?"

"Where are you going with this?"

"Someone said yes or no. There's always a gatekeeper."

"That's it?" Victor took on the gravity of a physician delivering a grim prognosis. "You're fucked."

"Maybe you'd like to elaborate on that."

"You can't go on pretending that you're an investigator."

"I've been doing it for years."

"Did they leave your gun?"

"Yes."

"You're being set up."

"Possibly."

"You are so fucked. You have no authority and no protection, just enemies. What are you looking for? Blood on the sidewalk and a round of applause?"

Arkady didn't know, although he thought a little clarity might do.

"The door is open," Arkady heard, and ventured in.

Wrapped in a silk robe, Madame Isa Spiridona, choreographer of the Club Nijinsky, reclined on a chaise longue with one arm free to reach her opium and brandy. Her apartment overlooked the Moscow River but it could have overlooked the Seine, with excellent copies of French antiques in tulipwood veneer and velvet-covered chairs. A dash of silk flowers. Inscribed photos of Colette, Coco and Marlene on a table. Photos of a young Spiridona dancing with Rudy and Baryshnikov on a grand piano. Photos covering the walls as if she were a person with no faith in her memory.

"Please forgive me if I don't rise. They say that dancers live a short time *en pointe* and a long time in pain. It was a brutal system, but it worked, didn't it? We had beauty and dancers. I suppose that's why you're here. To ask about Vera?"

"Yes."

"More questions about the Club Nijinsky."

"One more." He sat because one question always led to another. Stand and you're halfway out the door. "Who runs the auditions for the Nijinsky dancers?"

"I do. I am the choreographer."

"And there are many talented dancers who would like to be Nijinsky dancers?"

"Yes."

"And want nothing more than to audition for you?"

"Yes."

"Then why settle for a not very good dancer like Vera?"

"She had other qualities."

"Such as?"

"She was a charming individual. It came through in her dancing. It's something you can't teach."

"Do you mind if I turn up the lights?" He was at the switch before she could object, then returned and placed a snapshot before Spiridona.

"Do you remember Inna Ustinova? She was a yoga instructor. She wanted to be a Nijinsky dancer."

"Of course I remember her. She was too old. She would hang around the club, looking for a shoulder to cry on."

"Did she find any?"

"No. People here are professionals. I told her to go back to her yoga mats. I felt terrible when she was killed. Found by a dog. How horrible, how awful that must have been."

Arkady wasn't listening. What he had not noticed when the lights were low was a framed, dramatically dark poster of a young dancer with golden hair, the same boy that Arkady had seen drained of blood on a table in the morgue. On a salver was a stack of programs for different ballets.

She followed his eye. "My son, Roman."

"He dances too?"

"He did until he injured himself. Last week Roman called to say that he and his friend Sergei were going on a trip. Yesterday, Sergei called to say that Roman had gone on alone."

This was more than Arkady had bargained for. He had not

come as a messenger to tell this woman that her son was dead. Dead and burned under another name, yet.

"Where to?"

"I don't know. I try not to get in Roman's way. He suffers from depression but the doctors say I should let him hit bottom. What does that mean, 'hit bottom'?"

Roman Spiridon had certainly done that. Hit bottom and continued to the center of the earth. Not even as himself, but under another man's name.

Arkady remembered Madame Borodina's voice, as dry as kindling.

"Burn him."

Although the church condemned cremation, the state provided the option. Rolled him into a furnace with flames hot enough to melt gold, pulverized his ashes and bones and delivered them in a screw-top canister to the hands of Borodina. Where to, then? There was a choice of parks—Siloviki, Gorky or Ismailova—where ashes could be dumped. Or lobbed into a trash bin or poured like flour into the river.

"Sergei who?"

"Borodin."

"Sergei Borodin called instead of your son? To reassure you, but not tell you where they were going?"

"Sergei said he had to come back to pick up his book."

"What book would that be?"

"There on the desk. I'm waiting for him to pick it up."

On a Louis XIV desk was a well-worn paperback entitled *The Diary of Vaslav Nijinsky*, which sounded pretty innocent to Arkady. He flipped through the pages to see whether anything fell out.

"Do you mind if I borrow this?"

"Sergei is coming for it."

"Then he can come to me."

She didn't have the willpower to refuse him. Her attention gravitated to the opium layout, a lacquered tray inlaid with silver dragons and mother-of-pearl. A resinous "pill" nested in the bowl of a slender ivory pipe.

"Sometimes God's gifts were given to the wrong person."

"If Borodin is such a great dancer, why is he swinging on a wire at the Club Nijinsky instead of dancing with the Bolshoi?"

Spiridona asked, "How do I put this? Dancing is an intimate affair. The women don't like the way Sergei handled them."

"Too soft? Too hard?"

"Like chickens in a butcher shop."

23

Maya imagined herself on a golden escalator that reached up to the clouds. Her baby was just a few steps ahead. For some reason Maya could not close the distance or see what awaited them but she was sure it would be better than what they left behind.

"How old are you, my dear? In Pakistan, you would already be married and have a baby on your hip. Your breasts are full. That is exciting to a man, but leave the nursing and mess to someone else. No, let me undress you. It is my pleasure. I will fold everything neatly. My God, you are more beautiful every moment. Our mutual friend Yegor was not overstating the case. Do you like this place? It's an office of another friend, very important man. Pakistani, but the sofa is very comfortable, don't you think? Nice paintings if you could see them. Everything totally modern. Champagne on ice. Minibar. Would you like a drink? Up to you. Since it's Sunday we have all night and the entire building. The shaved head is curiously erotic, as if you had revealed everything to me. As you can see, I cannot hide the fact that I am not in the best of shape. When I came here as a student thirty years ago, I was thin as a reed. This is what Russian cooking does. My wife, bless her, is a wretched cook. I call her my wife although we're not really married. I don't know what Russians have against spices. Also I don't exercise nearly enough. A man my size should exercise. It's incumbent on him or he'll go to fat as I have. But I have to spend all day and night in the kiosk or my workers will rob me blind. Look at this. I haven't been this hard in ten years. Do you mind being kissed? I'll turn the lights down and you can pretend that you are having sex with the handsomest man in the world. If you touch me I'll explode. Really, really. Oh no, oh no, oh no. See? That comes from being deprived. But I've more to spare. I will run to the men's room and be immediately back. Give me one minute. It will be even better. Less urgent."

He whistled "Whistle While You Work" while he padded down the hall in bare feet. Everyone in the city was whistling the same tune; it was in the air. In the men's room he wiped himself, pinched the fat around his waist, shined a smile at the mirror to check his teeth. He didn't mind the interruption. In fact, the longer the better. His penis hung loose but not defeated, he thought.

The office lights were still low when he returned and he moved cautiously between tables and chairs to preserve his shins and whispered her name, almost cooing. When the lights suddenly went up, he found himself in the company of two men in coveralls, work boots and surgical gloves. Except for the gloves, the visitors looked like a pair of auto mechanics. A grocery bag stood on the coffee table and for a second he thought he might have strayed into the wrong office, but there was the comfortable sofa with the girl's imprint still on it. His clothes lay on the desk by a scarf of Maya's, but she was gone.

"Excuse me."

"Don't get dressed."

"Sit down."

The other man inserted a chair in back of Ali's knees. It was sit or fall.

Ali remained calm. This was an extortion racket and these two were the heavies. They seemed cast from the same rough mold, the difference being a dent here or there. With their flat voices and deep-set eyes, they played their roles convincingly.

"You've caught me fair and square. There is no need for further dramatics. How much are you asking?"

One man showed Ali a poster with Maya's face.

"Is this the girl?"

"Yes. See, whatever you want to know I will freely tell you." Ali believed it was important to establish a positive atmosphere while not exhibiting too much curiosity. He had been robbed in the kiosk half a dozen times and he had learned that panic was everyone's enemy. These two seemed professional, which was reassuring. Description-wise, both had nondescript hair, thin lips, no smile and the kind of beard that looked like a blue mask. Rather than ask them their names, he labeled the slightly larger man "Mr. Big" and the slightly thinner man "Mr. Little."

So it was Mr. Little who asked, "Where is she?"

"I have no idea. Does it matter? She's done her bit."

Mr. Big picked up the scarf and lifted it to his nose.

Ali nodded. "Yes, a delicious smell. She's a little siren. She was here only a minute ago, but now she's gone. That's God's truth."

He expected them to ask where to. Instead, they poked around the office and checked out the contents of the minibar. Felt the warm sofa.

Ali said, "I expected to see her when I returned from the men's, not you gentlemen."

"How about the baby?" Mr. Little moved behind Ali.

Ali had to twist in his chair. "She never mentioned a baby."

"How were her tits?"

"I observed that they were full like a nursing mother's. But she never mentioned a baby."

"Arms back."

"I am feeling somewhat exposed. Do you mind if I get dressed first?"

"Not yet."

"This is really not necessary."

Ali allowed himself to be handcuffed around the back of the chair. He was still ready to deal.

"She was here a minute ago, but you have no idea where she's headed?"

"With Yegor, obviously. May I get dressed now? This is no way to negotiate."

"Who's negotiating?"

The silence that followed was unnerving.

"This is not extortion?"

"Do we look like extortionists?"

No, Ali thought. He wished they did.

Mr. Big said, "If Yegor was out of the picture, where would she go?"

"I truly wish I could help you." Ali was calm. He'd been beaten by Russians before and suffered broken ribs just for walking down the street. They would find out that he could take punishment.

"From the kiosk you see everything, don't you?"

"No one can keep track of everything. People come and go all the time. It's Three Stations."

Mr. Little and Mr. Big communicated with a look that made Ali suck up his testicles.

"As I said before, I am not totally without funds. If you give me a figure to start with . . ." Ali's voice died off as Mr. Little took a box of see-through food wrap from the shopping bag and pulled off the opening strip. He fed plastic wrap through a slot in the lid, which he tucked next to a strip of saw-toothed metal. Where was the food? Ali wondered.

"Have you been wrapped before?" Mr. Big asked.

"Wrapped?"

"I'll take that as a no. It's simple. I am going to ask you where to find this girl and her baby. If you give us no answer or a wrong answer, we will wrap your head."

These were all scare tactics, Ali thought. Nobody did such things.

"We'll demonstrate. Are you claustrophobic?"

"No, sir."

"We'll see."

It took two people, one to hold the first turn of food wrap and another to circle with the box and unreel more. The tape was clear plastic. Ali could see through it and witness the whole operation in the reflection of the office window. Air was totally cut off. He nodded to indicate he got the idea but they continued to wrap until he was covered from his neck to the top of his head.

"It's important not to panic," said Mr. Little. "The faster your heart rate the faster you use up oxygen."

The wrap got tighter and molded itself to Ali's face. He wanted to protest that this was more than a demonstration, but his mouth was wrapped and muffled. In the reflection of the window he wore a silver helmet and rocked from side to side.

"Ali, relax! You have five minutes to go."

Five minutes? They misjudged! They must have thought they'd leave a little air! No, no, no, no! He rocked hard enough to lift himself and the chair clear of the floor. Banged his chin against his chest. Felt his lungs and chest begin to cave, a roar rise up in his ears and his vision go dark.

When Ali was conscious again, he was still handcuffed to

the chair but the plastic wrap had been removed, rolled into a ball and tossed into a wastebasket.

"Disposable," said Mr. Little.

Mr. Big asked, "Who needs the rack or the Spanish Inquisition when there's a roll of food wrap in the kitchen?" It was a philosophical proposition, not a question.

"Would you like some vodka?" Mr. Little poured vodka into Ali as if he were filling a gas tank. Ali drank in gulps, eager to be stunned.

"Back to business," said Mr. Little. "Where did the girl go?"

"Please, I have a family, small children and aged parents in Pakistan who have no other means of support."

"You putrid shit. What were you doing with your little whore, writing letters home?"

"I was weak. I was tempted and fell."

"Where would the girl go?"

"I swear I don't know."

"Last chance."

"Please."

Mr. Big ripped off a section of plastic wrap and at its touch to Ali's cheek, he jumped, chair and all.

"Genius. Everybody calls him Genius but his real name is Zhenya. I don't know his last name but he is often in the company of a prosecutor's investigator, Renko."

"Where?"

"The boy is always around Three Stations. You can't miss him; he hustles chess in the waiting rooms. I'll point him out to you. You don't need to wrap me anymore."

"Wrap you? Like what, a leftover piece of cheese? You must think we're fucking barbarians."

"No, not really but . . . I didn't know what to think."

Mr. Big slapped Ali on the back. "You should have seen your face. Come on. We'll take you down in the service elevator."

Ali laughed. He was unsteady after the handcuffs were removed and he dressed clumsily because of the vodka. And because when the elevator came he had to step over Yegor's body. The screw-off pool-cue butt that had been Yegor's scepter and cudgel was stuffed into his mouth. Ali couldn't stop laughing.

24

"Why did you wait so long to call?" Arkady asked Zhenya.

"She didn't want to involve the police."

"Why not? Three days ago we could have turned the city inside out. Today? No one would lift a finger. Is she deaf?"

"No." Although for all the attention Maya gave Arkady, she might have been. The windows of the car were fogged with condensation on which she drew a happy face.

The longer they waited for Victor, the more questions Arkady had for Zhenya.

Who was this girl?

How old was she?

Where was she from?

How could she lose a baby?

Did Zhenya ever actually see a baby?

Did anyone besides the girl ever see a baby?

Maya was mute. She hated Zhenya's so-called friend, Arkady. Zhenya may have lied to her, but he was the only one who had the nerve to walk into a building in search of her and lead her down the stairs while the two men in the elevator were busy stuffing Yegor into a body bag. It took her a moment to realize that the investigator was asking her directly, "Did you recognize the yellow station wagon?"

"No."

"From where?"

"I told you. Nowhere."

"Did you recognize the two men?"

They were the men she called the Catchers.

"No."

"They seemed to know you." He passed back the poster of her that the two men had been circulating. She let her forehead rest on the coolness of the backseat window and answered in a dreamy tone that she had never seen them before.

"And the Pakistani?"

"No."

"You never bought anything at his kiosk?"

"No."

Zhenya said the last they saw of the kiosk clerk, he was being dumped in the Volvo and covered with a tarp.

"Did they see you?"

"On the street," Zhenya said. "That's how I found her, by following their car."

"Did they get a good look at you?"

"Yes."

"What did they look like?"

"Average. Average everything."

"Nothing else?"

The word Zhenya came up with was "Brothers."

Victor climbed into the Lada and said the office site was microscopically clean.

"Anyway, who is going to report that a runaway like Yegor is missing, or give a damn about a Pakistani? Not to mention, the age of consent is still sixteen. Do you think men who have sex with children are going to report suspicious activity?"

Arkady said to Zhenya, "You know better. You should have called."

It wasn't until they reached the richly dressed shop windows of Tverskaya Street that Maya realized the investigator hadn't taken her and Zhenya to the police.

Arkady remembered that his cupboard was bare and sent Victor and Zhenya dashing through the rain into a food emporium. Also, Arkady wanted a private word with Maya. He had not appreciated at first how close to the edge the girl was. He wasn't prepared for her. The streets of Moscow were lined with Viking women. Maya was small and graceful and her shaved head added vulnerability. He could see why Zhenya was senseless around her.

"You want to talk?" Maya said.

"That's right. Just you and me."

"Okay. Let's hear what kind of bullshit you come up with."

He thought she might be a good judge of character. He wondered what kind of self-justification had been poured into her ears by men paying for sex with a child.

"If you love your baby so much, why won't you try to find her?"

"Won't look for her? All I've done for the last three days is search the stations again and again."

"I know. But that's punishing yourself, not searching for the baby anywhere but Three Stations. There's much more to Moscow. It confuses me because I believe you're a good mother."

"How would you know that?"

"Because you're suffering."

"You don't know anything."

"Then let me guess. You're a runaway, you're a prostitute and you're running for your life."

She asked, "What else?"

"You hid the baby in something it could breathe in, maybe a basket, and probably traveled second class at night. Pickpockets and confidence artists work as teams. One bumps you while the other lifts your money. Or one threatens you and the other comes to your rescue."

"Auntie Lena chased a soldier who was bothering me."

"Afterward, did Auntie Lena give you anything to drink?"

"Yes."

"It had knockout powder. Once you drank that, you didn't have a chance."

"I asked people later if they saw a woman with a baby get off the train."

"By then the soldier had joined her, only he didn't look like a soldier and she didn't look like anybody's Auntie Lena. They looked like an ordinary family on a trip. That would be my guess."

"And . . ."

"And the two men you saw in the elevator with Yegor are after you. I'm not sure whether you've seen them before, but you know what they are. Once in a while a girl escapes. Then someone has to go after her and not only catch her, but make an example of her, so other girls won't try."

"They take pictures."

"I've seen them."

She had visions of women hanging from a meat hook, set on fire, floating facedown in a swimming pool.

"They tell us it's useless to escape because they're everywhere. Not only in Russia. They never stop looking and sooner or later they find you. I could be on the North Pole and they would find me. Is that true?"

"Pretty much."

"You're cheery."

"Sorry."

"What about the . . ."

"The bodies? I don't care about them, I care about you. They're dead, you're alive. There are two professional killers after you. We have to keep you as far from this scene as possible."

"I could do it if I knew Katya survived."

"That's the baby's name?"

"Katya. She has a blue blanket with a design of baby chicks and a birthmark on the back of her neck if you lift her hair. I haven't settled on a last name yet."

"Keep your options open."

"My own is Pospelova. Remember that later." She smiled. "Maya Pospelova was here."

They spread a bounty of cheese, bread, red caviar, chocolates and coffee on Arkady's kitchen table. He kept his eye on Maya. Surrendering her name seemed to have relieved her mind, as if a decision had been made. Her serenity worried Arkady, that and her use of the word "later." Arkady saw her wrist. He suspected that while Maya had little in the way of Plan A, she always had a trusty Plan B in the form of a razor blade.

Meanwhile Maya was entertained by Victor's stories. According to Victor, the art of the suicide note had deteriorated.

"A suicide tweet is not the same thing."

"Don't you think that people who believe in love are happier?"

"It depends on who you are. Arkady falls in love with the regularity of spawning salmon, whereas I have incredibly high standards, yet we're equally miserable. It's become a national crisis. No romance, no little Russians, no army. That's why Putin played Cupid."

"I don't remember that," said Maya. There hadn't been newspapers at the bordello.

"He declared a Holiday of Love with bouquets for all the married women who came to Red Square. The weather was a little cool, a little cloudy. Putin wants everything perfect, so he salts the clouds.

"We do it for every parade. Planes go back and forth seeding clouds. The seeds are pellets of silver iodide and liquid nitrogen compacted into a block of cement powder. Each block, as an airman throws it out of the plane, explodes into a puff of dust. All but one."

Arkady said, "It's a shame you don't have children just so you could terrify them."

Victor continued unabashed. "One block stays together and plunges to the city from ten thousand meters like, well, a block of cement. To the pilots it appears that the block is aimed directly at the Kremlin. Options are considered. Try to shoot the block and make it disintegrate, at the risk of mowing down dozens of mothers in Red Square? Ram the block, at the risk of bringing down the plane? Do nothing and perhaps witness the most unusual political assassination in history? Of course they ended up doing nothing and the block came down in an apartment building nowhere near and tore through a roof and three bathrooms before coming to rest in a tub. I like to think of it as 'Putin's Arrow.'"

Arkady was restless. He didn't know why. He fancied he heard the click of a latch out on the landing.

"Excuse me." Arkady got up and went to the hall. Music was playing faintly in Anya's apartment. A samba.

Arkady knocked. When there was no answer, he rang the bell. He knocked again, then knelt and saw light under the door sash. The door was locked, but he carried a credit card for jimmying door locks.

Victor came out from Arkady's apartment. "What's the matter?"

"Tell Zhenya and Maya to stay there."

Arkady shoved the card in between the door and the jamb. A primitive method, but the door eased open.

The layout of Anya's apartment was a mirror of Arkady's, only hers was furnished with cheerful silk flowers, painted chairs and a buoyant disarray. Art covered the living-room walls. Mainly retro Socialist Realism painted with a smirk. The kitchen was dominated by a café-size espresso machine with brass fittings. There was little evidence of cooking besides a microwave oven and a list of phone numbers for take-out food. An empty glass stood in the sink.

Arkady called out Anya's name. No answer.

Victor pulled latex gloves from his pocket. Arkady wondered how many men walked around with latex gloves in their pocket, just in case.

Anya's office was a research center of book stacks, files, computer gear and photographs of Alexander Vaksberg pinned to a corkboard. Arkady's heart pounded, as if saying, *Getting warmer*.

"In here," Victor said. "The bedroom."

Arkady had the general impression of a bright, messy bedroom with artwork and photos. He focused on Anya. She was on her back between a bureau and the bed, her nightgown pushed up to her waist. Her right ankle was over the left and her arms stretched back and gently touched, a perfect demonstration of the fifth position. She had no pulse or respiration and her skin was blue.

GOD IS SHIT was spray-painted on the wall above her. The paint was still wet and smelled of acetone. Victor turned where he stood as if they had fallen into a cave.

Arkady read the emergency bracelet on her wrist.

Milk.

Some people were fatally allergic to peanuts or shellfish. One taste and their immune system reacted so violently that they went into anaphylactic shock: their hearts stopped and their airways shut tight. Anya was blue for lack of oxygen. But there was death and there was death, and in between was a netherworld where the brain was on its own. He knelt beside her to look into her eyes. Her pupils still had their shape, not collapsed, and when he shined a penlight at them, they drew tight.

"She's still alive." *So far*, he could have added. Without oxygen, brain cells started dying at two minutes. At four minutes half the brain was dead matter. She would certainly be dead by the time an ambulance arrived.

Arkady had his moment of clarity. Anya didn't eat, she drank coffee.

The emergency kit—a white plastic box with a red cross—was the only item in the refrigerator. The contents of the kit were a plastic mask attached to a rubber bulb and an EpiPen preloaded with adrenaline.

Arkady exposed the needle and thrust it into Anya's thigh. Instantly, she jerked and her heart began to beat.

He slipped the mask over Anya's face. Her heart would race until it dropped like a dead horse unless she started to breathe. Each squeeze of the mask's rubber bulb forced air into Anya's mouth. Her lips were purple and although it was like trying to animate clay, he maintained a rhythm of squeeze and release, squeeze and release, every five seconds as if her heart were in his hand.

"How long are you going to try this?" Victor asked.

Arkady heard a gasp and caught Zhenya and Maya standing in the doorway. Maya's hand was over her mouth.

Victor whispered, "The longer it takes, the less likely she can be revived. You can't raise the dead."

She wasn't dead, Arkady thought. He wouldn't allow it.

"Arkady." Victor tried to pull him up.

"Wait," Maya said.

Squeeze and release. Squeeze and release.

Anya's first breath was harsh and ugly. Arkady continued to pump until her respiration was steady and the blue cast of her skin gave way to pink.

25

Arkady had put Anya in his bed. Light hurt her eyes, and he had turned off all the lights except a reading lamp that he turned low. He expected her to fall into a deep sleep, but adrenaline was still racing through her system.

"Half the time I think I'm dead again."

"You had a traumatic experience. I would guess that being dead, even for a short time, qualifies as traumatic."

"It wasn't what I expected."

"No white light?"

"Nothing."

"No family or friends?"

"Zero."

"Let's talk about whoever tried to kill you."

"I don't know who it was. I don't remember anything from this afternoon on." Anya shifted for a better view of Arkady. "You knew what to do. You've seen someone in shock before. Was it a woman?"

"Yes. I didn't know what to do then. I do now."

Overlap was the last thing he wanted. No spilling of memory from one woman to another. Yes, he had helplessly witnessed anaphylactic shock before. This time at least he had a chance to save someone. Arkady had taken no chances. He had concentrated on the bulb and mask as if they were a rope out of an abyss, and hadn't even noticed when life first began to creep back into her body.

"This was different, someone tried to kill you."

"They did kill me."

"But you're alive now."

"Maybe."

"I heard two separate sets of footsteps leave your apartment, and you say you didn't have any guests?"

"I don't remember. Could I have a cigarette now?"

"Definitely not. Somebody left a glass with a residue of milk in your kitchen sink. Can you tell me who that somebody might be?"

"I'm a journalist. Don't you know it's open season on journalists?"

"And you don't want to call in the police."

"Why should I when I have you?"

"Well, I have been dismissed. How much I can help is debatable."

"I'll take my chances." In a different tone, she asked, "How long was I dead?"

"Comatose."

"Dead," she insisted. "In other words, am I swimsuit ready? Sasha Vaksberg has asked me to go to his dacha tomorrow." She pulled back the sheet from her leg to examine the dark bruise left by Arkady and the needle.

"I don't think you've lost anything," Arkady said.

"The dacha is enormous. Sasha has two swimming pools,

tennis courts and a ring for horses. Sometimes I think he pays people just to walk around."

"I'm sure it's very grand."

"You think I should go."

"You might be safer there than here."

"Do you have a dacha?"

"A shack." He tried to return to the attack. "As a journalist, do you keep an appointment book?"

"Is your shack on a river or a lake?"

"Just a pond."

"Describe it."

"Ordinary."

"In what way?"

"A cabin with three rooms, half of a kitchen, bad paintings, a stone fireplace, a family of hedgehogs under the porch, a canoe and a rowboat on a dock. My father was a general, but after enough vodka, he thought he was an admiral."

"That doesn't sound so bad. Was I dressed?"

"Excuse me?"

"When you found me, was I dressed?"

"Not completely."

"How did I look? Is blue in fashion?"

"You're asking the wrong man. What about Sasha Vaksberg? He must have called in reinforcements by now. He could have given you a hundred bodyguards."

"Maybe he would have. He's an unpredictable man."

Anya took in the high ceiling, a monstrous armoire, light patches on the wall where photographs and paintings had been removed.

"Did you grow up here? It must have been something at one time."

"It was where the 'party elite' lived, and it was a great honor to be assigned an apartment like this. On the other hand, it was full of false walls and secret passageways for the KGB to listen. And once a month or so, some famous face would disappear. So it was an honor with a certain risk. While no one could refuse to live in such a luxurious establishment, they always kept a suitcase packed."

"Did they ever listen in on your father?"

"He was very accommodating. He would tell the agents his itinerary for the day. And night."

"Did it affect you to live in such a haunted house?"

"I'm embarrassed to say no. I did find the wall that the agent sat behind. I had a rubber ball and I bounced it against the wall a hundred times, two hundred times."

"I don't think you were cut out to be a policeman."

"It's a little late in the day to learn that. What does it mean, 'God is shit'?"

She yawned. "I have no idea."

He said, "I understand 'God is dead.' 'God is shit' escapes me."

He waited but Anya had fallen into a deep, enviable sleep. Arkady got as comfortable as he could in the chair and dipped into the book he had taken from Madame Spiridona. The diary of a ballet dancer promised to be tame enough. *After the triumph in Paris, we opened in Monte Carlo . . .* That sort of thing.

Instead, the pages fell open to *God is Dog, Dog is God, Dog is Shit, God is Shit, I am Shit, I am God.*

And *I am a beast and a predator . . . everyone will be afraid of me and commit me to a lunatic asylum. But I don't care. I am not afraid of anything. I want death.*

26

Itsy had picked a trailer with a stove that, however small and miserly, kept her family warm. She swaddled the baby in her blue comforter and hardly gave her a chance to cry before a bottle was put to her mouth.

Itsy emphasized safety. Girls should beg in pairs. Boys might beg alone but in sight of each other. The problem was that the rain made any begging impossible; people lowered their eyes and bulled ahead. Although Itsy had a rule about not sniffing glue, it was difficult to enforce after hours of idleness. The silence was stranger for hearing through the wall the rush of passengers and the coming and going of trains. Sometimes a locomotive sounded as if it were coming right to their laps. The PA announced arrivals and departures in round, unintelligible tones.

Going to the children's shelter was out of the question. Not because the people who ran it were mean; most were kind. But the family would be split up according to age and sex and Tito would probably be shot.

Mainly to give the kids something to do, Itsy took them to the video arcade behind Leningrad Station, leaving the sleeping baby in the care of Emma, Tito and the two oldest boys, Leo and Peter. Itsy was barely out the door when the boys put Tito on a leash and took paper bags and cans of air freshener from their day packs. They dragged a mattress out of the trailer to sit on.

Emma piped up: "I know what you're doing."

"But you're not going to tell anyone, are you?" Leo said.

"Depends. Itsy won't be happy."

Peter said, "In case you haven't noticed, Itsy's not here. We're in charge."

"And we're bored," said Leo. "Everyone else has fun while we babysit you and the brat. Here." He offered her a cigarette.

"I can't. Because of the baby."

Peter smirked. "That's if you're pregnant. Jesus, you're stupid."

Emma, affronted, climbed into the trailer. If boys were so smart, how come they didn't know how to change a diaper? She considered the argument won.

Outside the trailer, Leo and Peter sprayed the freshener inside their paper bags, lifted the bags like cups of gold and breathed deeply. Almost instantaneously aerosol chemistry entered the bloodstream and breached the brain.

Euphoria and warmth flowed over the boys. Forgetting that he was in a railway repair shed, Leo remarked on the fading light. Fading but profound in a pre-Creation way. Because in that emptiness was, well, everything. The entire universe fit into the palm of his hand.

Peter said he was going to get his shit together. He had a plan to get off of the streets, study the martial arts, join the army, win some medals and become Putin's bodyguard. He would need his parents' consent to enlist early. That should be no problem; they would sign anything for a bottle of vodka.

A power sweeper rolled into the shed. The rider was a Tajik from the station chasing paper cups and soda cans. He not only had a headlight; he aimed a flashlight into the corners of the shed.

What the boys saw was a Mongol on a shaggy horse, a warrior of the Golden Horde in plate armor traveling from another time with arrows of blinding light. He maneuvered around the trench and approached the trailer and played the beam over Leo and Peter, over the bags and cans loose in their hands.

Tito the dog had been trained not to bark. He approached to the limit of his leash with his ears back and eyes burning while the warrior floated to the stack of fruit crates that Itsy's group had been breaking up to use as firewood. The pile was halfway down. He lifted a crate and examined a taut plastic sack of brown Afghan heroin. He removed and counted every sack, then replaced each sack and crate as it was.

When he was done he returned to the trailer. He lifted Peter by his forelock as if he were lifting a rat by the tail and slid open the blade of a box cutter. Peter's eyes rolled back. The Tajik's gaze only happened to follow and catch Emma at the window before she ducked down. Jostled, the baby began to cry.

Emma didn't need to think what to do next. It was as if a devil took over her body and she found herself functioning with cold selfishness, placing the baby as bait at one end of the trailer and crouching behind cots at the other. She was astonished and horrified at herself, but there was no stopping. While the Tajik entered the trailer and went to the baby, Emma slipped out the door and hid in the trench. The baby cried and cried. Emma closed her eyes, held her breath and clamped her legs together tight to keep from peeing.

The baby's crying abruptly stopped. Emma was sure she was next. Any second the devil would find her in the trench and slit her throat. Eventually she became aware that the sweeper

was gone and Leo and Peter were drowsily comparing halluci-
nations.

"Tough. You missed out," Peter told Emma.

"It was wild," said Leo.

Emma said nothing. She rushed to the rear of the trailer.
There the baby was sucking on a small, leather amulet like
those worn by Tajik women passing through Three Stations.
Inside the amulet would be a quotation from the Koran as protection for the bearer.

27

★

The café at Kazansky Station was becoming a regular haunt for Arkady and Victor. Arkady wondered how many times in a row Victor could escape paying the check.

"At this point you're not just challenging Zurin, you're taking on the apparatus of the state, and the state may have the brain of a sea slug but it reacts to threats and it protects itself. Certain people will come to your apartment and they won't be boys with stage fright and they will break some bones. And what do you do? You pick a fight with Zurin. By the way, when is your billionaire friend, Vaksberg, going to pick up his car? I got a call from the evidence clerk. It's pretty shot up."

"He'll probably just buy himself a new one. I'm not going to drive all the way to the highway to look at holes in a car. Is that your eau de cologne I smell?"

This was a twist; Victor used to drink eau de cologne.

"It's for men," Victor said.

"Some, maybe."

Victor lit a cigarette and played with a matchbox.

"May I?" Arkady took the matchbox away.

Although the box was yellow with age, a portrait of a young Anna Furtseva on the cover was unmistakable. All that was missing was the combustible wolfhound.

"You went back."

"She called and said she had found a photograph she wanted me to have. That's it in your hand. It was a joke, just a means of invitation. When I got there she had made borscht and put out smoked fish and bread and beer. Then she gave me a corduroy jacket barely worn. Some toiletries that were never used. It was like visiting Granny."

"A granny who wants you to shoot her downstairs neighbors. And the jacket fit?"

"Yes. She knew my size."

"It sounds that way."

Arkady got in the car, turned on the engine and realized that he had no place to go. He was a former senior investigator. He could try to pursue the killer of Vera but he had no authority. The case would turn into the hobby of a harmless eccentric.

He had parked in the ranks of official cars in front of the station, one of the small perks that would be denied him in the future. He would also have to surrender his blue roof light and the right to use the official lane.

Brooding, it took him a minute to notice that Anya was arguing with a militia officer at the station's Oriental double door. On one side, a militia officer; on the other, a dozen kids in cloth caps and ragged sweaters, their wrists and necks ringed with dirt. They gathered around Anya like cats at a bowl of milk. The militia officer pushed them aside to get at the athletic bag. Arkady got out of the Lada as a tug-of-war over the bag developed. It was the sort of thing, he thought, that could end badly.

Half of him wanted to walk away. Instead, he waded through the crush and whispered in an official tone, "Let her go or I will have your balls on a plate."

The officer automatically stepped back because people who spoke softly in such situations were used to giving orders.

Arkady followed up by asking Anya, "What's the problem?"

"I only asked to look in the bag," the officer said.

"He wants to steal my bag."

Arkady said, "I will open the bag."

Anya burned, but she handed over the bag. He unzipped it to display energy bars, medical kits, condoms, soap and woolen socks.

"Satisfied?" Anya asked.

"You're going to sell these," the officer said.

"No, it's for children, homeless children. The Vaksberg Foundation gives them clothes, blankets, bedrolls. It's hardly going to improve the welfare of homeless children, but it shows them that somebody cares."

"To give away."

"Yes, to give away."

The officer went off disappointed, already searching for fresh prey.

Arkady pulled Anya into the station.

"What are you doing out of bed?"

"You think I should lie there all day long?"

"Yes," said Arkady. "Bed rest is the standard treatment for almost getting killed. Why are you acting this way? What happened?"

Street children filtered back in and she tried to say nothing, but the words came out: "Vaksberg has been skimming."

"You just found this out?"

"This morning. He's bankrupt."

"But he's a billionaire."

"Billionaires go bankrupt all the time. This morning I was trying to write. I read a Vaksberg Group memo I was never supposed to see. That's the danger of giving a writer total access. It was from Sasha to the chief financial officer instructing him how to inflate the valuation of the company as if all his casinos were operating. He's bankrupt."

"Then how did he fund the luxury fair?"

"There's only one way. He paid out what he took in. He's been skimming for months."

"What are you going to do?"

"Nothing. Nobody would give to any children's fund again. They want a reason not to."

"What can I do?"

"Oh, yes. You can advise ten-year-old girls how to put a condom on a grown man's dick." Louder she said, "Everyone wave to Uncle Arkasha because he's going away."

At first Arkady simply drove to escape Anya's scorn. Then he drove aimlessly because he didn't want to be anywhere.

Except the dacha.

The dacha passed to him from his father was no more than two hours from the city. It was a ramshackle cabin overgrown with lilacs and brambles but it had springwater and a path through a stand of black pines to a lake not much larger than a pond. An elderly neighbor looked in from time to time to check the house for leaks or hornet nests. Boris had to be almost ninety now. Whenever he discovered that Arkady had arrived, he would show up at the door as busy as a badger in a long scarf carrying a tray of pickles and bread and a jar of *samogon*. Moonshine. Arkady always invited him in for a glass. Eyes shining, Boris would pour *samogon* until it quivered with surface tension above the brim of the glass.

"Such a small glass," he said every time. Later they would

walk to the church and visit his wife's grave. The cemetery was a maze of white crosses and black wrought iron fences, some grave sites so "landlocked" that they were beyond reach.

Boris would set a jar of pansies or daisies at his wife's cross. He changed the flowers every day in summer. There was a bench at the grave site so a person could really visit. Nothing had to be said aloud. In the winter Arkady thought of it as ice fishing with God. There were times, however, when he felt one with the world, when his breath was a cloud and the birches brushed one against the other like a line of dancers curtsying in turn.

Instead, he drove to a towed-vehicle yard on the Ring Road, where there were no trees, only lamps and rain and a system designed to create the greatest possible inconvenience for anyone retrieving a towed car. The master of the yard negotiated fines and bribes at the window of a caravan while car owners stood in the rain. Cars held as evidence in criminal cases were in a separate, abutting lot that was as still as a graveyard because there was no ransom to be made from cars going nowhere.

The guard recognized Arkady and waved him through. "Remember, anything you find has to be reported to me."

"Absolutely."

"She's all yours," the guard said, and trotted back to his post.

Sasha Vaksberg's Mercedes seemed to be sinking into the mire like an abandoned warhorse. Arkady counted five holes in the right rear fender and door. Otherwise, the car was practically new and likely to disappear if Vaksberg didn't claim it. A billionaire could just buy a new Mercedes like disposable tissue; use it once and throw it away.

There was nothing in the car's cabin, although Arkady went through the glove compartment, side and seat pockets, under the floor pads.

He opened the trunk. In the spare-tire well was his small reward, a ticket printed on paper so cheap it almost disintegrated in his hand. It was torn on the diagonal and said *Central Mosc—ticket #15–100 ru—* Ticket to what? A movie? The symphony? The circus? Belonging to Dopey or Vaksberg or his dead driver or bodyguard? Or the last person to change a tire? Arkady had no idea. The tease was worse than finding nothing. This was what he had come down to, a wet stub.

It began to rain heavily. Arkady waved as he passed through the gate. The guard waved back, thankful that he had not been beckoned from his miserable shelter.

Rain fell in sheets. Where water pooled, trucks pounded through and cars rooster-tailed. At the height of the downpour, the wiper came half off on Arkady's side of the windshield. Somehow the clip that attached the rubber blade to the wiper itself had come off. He turned off to the side of the road to reconnect it. What next? Arkady wondered. Snow? Frogs? Snow and frogs? He had only himself to blame. Once Victor mentioned the Mercedes, Arkady was compelled to examine it.

It wasn't a totally empty road. The blurred lights of an industrial park lurked a few kilometers ahead. There was plenty of room on the shoulder and Arkady worked by the light of the Lada's open door. The wiper clip was bent. The trick was to bend it back without snapping it off. He remembered the days when rain would cause general confusion as cars pulled off to put on their precious windshield wipers. In those days, a driver carried a whole toolbox.

Arkady needed a pair of needle-nose pliers he did not have. He felt that no one should attempt to drive Victor's Lada unless he was completely outfitted. Say a needle-nose pliers and an inflatable raft. That was what made life an adventure. He worked by the light of the open door and squinted at the oncoming high beams of a truck that straddled the shoulder of the road. He shielded his eyes. Someone's idea of a joke, Arkady told himself. He felt his whole body light up. Beyond shielding his eyes, he couldn't move. They would turn any second. Any second.

Arkady dove into the Lada. With a crack the door of the Lada went sailing. By the time he pulled himself up, all Arkady saw were taillights dissolving in the dark.

28

"Have you ever tried to carry a car door in the rain?" Arkady asked.

Victor said nothing, only circled his car in disbelief. It was parked outside in the morning sun at the upscale Patriarch's Pond militia station, virtually a "No Lada Zone."

Arkady said, "We're lucky the hinges were a clean break. The man at the body shop never saw one so . . . immaculate."

Victor said, "It's not my door. This door is held on by wires."

"It will need some work. The main thing is, it opens. Shuts, pretty much. They tried to match the color."

"A black door on a white car? Next time, why don't you just drive it off a cliff?"

"I was on the shoulder of the highway. Someone tried to run me over."

Arkady resisted the temptation to point out that Victor owned a car that already looked as though it had been driven over a cliff.

"I found this." He opened an envelope and shook out the half ticket from the trunk of Vaksberg's Mercedes.

Victor stared. "You got this? What is it?"

"A ticket of some kind."

"Is it?"

Arkady tried to think of something that would cheer Victor. "The wiper works."

Victor led Arkady to the squad room even as he shot Arkady a sharp glance. "You know kids race on that highway all the time. It could have been one of them getting out of control. Did you see them?"

"No."

"Did you report them?"

"No."

"Did you shoot at them at least?"

Victor had set up laptops and old-fashioned paper dossiers to search among the dead. Each disc held a thousand dossiers and each dossier held a detective's account, interviews, forensic photos and autopsies of women who died of unnatural and unsolved causes in and around Moscow over the last five years. Arkady eliminated domestic squabbles, which still left a crowd since more than twelve thousand Muscovites died of unnatural causes in a year.

Arkady drew a clumsy version of ballet positions.

Victor said, "I didn't know you were such a scholar of the dance."

"It's as if Vera wore a sign saying 'Victim Number Four.'"

"Or her limbs happened to lie in a way that you and you alone construe to be a ballet position. What any normal person would notice was her bare ass."

Victor took a halfhearted swat at a fly that was making a tour of the room's fly strips, plastic spoons and take-out cartons.

"You know this would make some sense if it would do anything for Vera. Her case is closed. There is no corpus and the chances of gaining a conviction without a body don't exist."

"Unless somebody confesses."

"No body, no show. All they have to do is outwait us."

"For a moment, assume I'm right, far-fetched as that may be. If you have a killer who is counting up to five bodies and he's reached five in his mind, he's going to disappear on us. He could go to ground for a year or two and then start all over again with a new set of dance partners."

"We're missing number three."

"That's right. So let's narrow the search to women eighteen to twenty-two, student, dancer, sexually molested, murdered, OD'd, unknown causes. Make it within the last two years before Vera."

"Just two?"

"If I'm right, this is a compulsive character. He doesn't have a Five-Year Plan. He can't wait that long."

He watched the fly make the arduous trek up the wall, across the ceiling and around a light fixture only to reach journey's end as a buzz on a ringlet of flypaper.

Arkady got home after midnight and found Anya sitting in the dark.

She said, "I wanted to apologize for how I acted at the train station."

"Well, you seem popular with the kids."

"But not with you."

"You were exhausted, you should have stayed here. Have you eaten today?" Arkady asked.

When she had to think, he went directly to the refrigerator and pulled out leftovers from the night before and put the kettle on for tea.

"I have no appetite," Anya said.

"Who would at this hour?" He sliced sausage and black bread.

"Can I stay one more night?"

"You can stay as long as you need. Did anyone see you when you were out?"

"Just the children. I won't snoop, if that's what you're worried about."

"I'm sure you have snooped. You probably opened every drawer in the apartment. You may have opened drawers that haven't been opened in years. Right now, the main thing is nobody sees you. While you're dead, you're safe."

"And when I want to be alive?"

"At the right time. What kind of car does Sergei Borodin drive?"

"A huge American car. Why do you ask?"

"Someone tried to run me down today." Arkady poured two cups of tea. "When a person tries to run me down, I want to know why. Is he a killer or a jealous lover? It makes a difference."

"Go to hell."

It was good, Arkady thought. Her color was back and she started to pick at her food.

"So you're still on the case," she said.

"It would help if we had a witness. You don't have any recollection who attacked you?"

"None."

"But you haven't answered my question."

"First tell me who you are sleeping with," Anya said. "Or is that none of my business?"

"It isn't. But to be fair, no one."

"The woman who was living here, the doctor . . ."

"Is in Africa. Or Asia."

"You and women," Anya said.

"Not a success story, I'm afraid."

"Why did she leave?"

"Because she wants to save the world. I don't."

"That's not who I see."

"Who do you see?" He expected a gibe.

"I see a man who didn't desert me."

Anya kissed him and pulled back.

"I'm sorry," she said.

"Please don't be."

Things were in motion, some secret word had been spoken, because they kissed again. There was still time for Arkady to walk away from a case he did not fathom and a woman he did not understand. He knew there was no case and no investigation. What were the chances of a happy outcome? He could stop now. Instead, he moved around the table and gathered her up. She was incredibly light and he discovered while her body was small it was deep enough for the rest of the world to disappear.

Afterward, still in bed, she dipped a sugar cube into her cup and sucked the sweet tea through.

29

As soon as Itsy saw the amulet in the baby's basket, she mo-
bilized the family, no matter that it was in the dark of night.
They had encroached on a Tajik cache of heroin hidden under
the crates they had been using as firewood for the trailer stove.
The amulet was an eviction notice. A parade of runaways with
a crying baby was likely to interest people. However, few people
were likely to be outside on such a damp night. Besides, the
baby had become too precious to Itsy to give up. She had little
concept of the long term. At heart she knew that the long term
did not apply to her. All she had were day-to-day survival skills
but she had no complaints. School, office, a comfortable old
age held no appeal for her. In many ways her life was perfect.

Leo and Peter lagged behind. They were in the heavy eyelids
phase of sniffing. Everyone had different stuff. Aerosol, model
glue or shoe polish. Itsy wanted the boys along because they
were big enough to provide some protection; otherwise, the
responsibility fell on Tito, who had trotted along one side of

the group and then the other until they reached Kazansky Station, where they huddled and waited for the boys to catch up. A three-week-old baby, even one as well swaddled as Itsy's, was not meant to be out in the damp and cold.

"The boys left their gear," Milka said.

Their sniffing gear, Itsy thought. Their stupid cans and bags.

"Stay here." Itsy handed the baby over to Emma.

Itsy ran back the way she had come, with every step rehearsing the things she was going to say to Leo and Peter when she found them.

The railway shed was a shadow set in a field of rails. She paused on the tracks to listen for a footfall or voice. Although she had a flashlight, she kept it dark. Her senses had been educated by living on the run and she saw the deeper, darker trench for undercarriage repairs, caught the scents of ashes and urine and heard the drip of rainwater from the open sleeve of a drainpipe. There was no sign of magical Tajik warriors astride either thunderclouds or floor sweepers. All the same, she was uneasy about being near Tajik goods.

The trailer stove still held embers and a diminishing nub of warmth. As Itsy maneuvered between bunk beds she remembered the grandiose plans she had had for a portable crib. It could still happen once she established a new base. It was just a matter of getting through the night.

Itsy smelled blood. She stepped down from the trailer and looked under the wheels. Then she returned to the lip of the trench and this time turned on the flashlight. Leo and Peter were facedown on the bottom of the trench, each with a hole of not much account in the back of the cranium. Their caps had been tossed in afterward. Itsy had promised Leo a new pair of used basketball shoes. A cigarette was still stylishly cocked behind Peter's ear, the cigarette he never smoked. A buzz in Itsy's head was faint at first but growing to monumental dimensions.

Her mother said, "Isabel is a beautiful name," and the flashlight died.

The second shot dropped Itsy into the trench and a pair of silhouettes took her place.

"And one more for good luck."

His gun made a dull pop.

There was a moment of quiet satisfaction, terminated by the sound of padded feet approaching fast.

"What's that?"

"A fucking dog."

Tito hit the nearer shooter chest-high. Both landed in the trench, the dog on top.

"Get him off me."

"Stay still." A second figure looked down from the edge of the trench.

"Off me."

"Don't move."

"God!"

"I don't have an angle."

"Mother of . . ."

"You have to stop moving."

"Neck."

The man on the edge aimed as best he could and fired. The tussling continued in a one-sided way.

"Ilya, you all right? Ilya?"

The second shooter found Itsy's flashlight and shined it into the trench.

His brother said nothing because his carotid artery was torn and the dog was pulling him without resistance one way and then the other. Blood everywhere.

"Ilya!"

As Tito looked up, his eyes lit. He dropped the man from his jaws and started for the steps, gathering speed as he came. The second shooter emptied the rest of his clip on the dog and was still squeezing the trigger when the animal rolled back down the steps, dead ten times over.

Decisions had to be made. In ordinary circumstances, the shooter would never leave his brother behind. Ilya had been a master at tying up loose ends. Dead, Ilya was the biggest loose end of all. Just the logistics. Getting Ilya to the Volvo or the Volvo to Ilya. Finding a cartridge for every round he had fired. Digging two more graves. For the sweat alone he deserved a bonus.

Something flitted across the shooter's face. An orange laser that moved as erratically as a butterfly came to rest on the nameplate of his coveralls. He felt the coolness of the air.

"Fucking Tajiks."

That much he figured out before the bullet hit.

30

Morning at a sobriety station meant the time had come for all the zombies to dress and shuffle out the door, for station attendants to hose the floor and remake the beds with rubber sheets, and for Swan, the medic, coming to the end of a twenty-four-hour shift, it was time to drop into a chair and light a cigarette as if his life depended on it. Swan was not quite a doctor and not quite a pirate. He talked with his eyes closed. "God is dog. Dog is God. God is shit."

"It's catchy," Arkady said. "I heard it a few days ago when I came for Sergeant Orlov."

"As long as they're not hurting themselves or anyone else, they can say what they want. We take care of our guests. If they're bleeding, we put on a plaster. If they throw up, we make sure they don't choke to death. We even saw the legs off their beds so they won't be injured if they fall out. They fall out of bed a lot. We also afford them privacy."

Surely such a bed had a future in the furniture department, Arkady thought. The "Moscow Model," for shorter falls.

"The station log?" he asked.

Swan lifted a ledger-size book from his desk.

The log was simple: name, time of admission, time of release, condition and, in some instances, in whose custody or to what hospital. The fine of 150 rubles for disorderly conduct was picayune, but demotion at the workplace and grief at home could be serious. A hundred dollars could make all that disappear and Arkady would have expected Sergei Borodin to take that route, yet there was his signature boldly written in ink. Admitted three nights before at 20:45, released 23:00. Arkady noticed that according to the log, Roman Spiridon was admitted at the same time.

"Borodin said he wanted privacy, and then he gets the ward in an uproar with his 'God is shit' routine. That's all I need, trouble with the church."

"Did Borodin get drunk often?"

"Who said he was drunk?"

"He admitted himself?"

"It's like any club. There are special arrangements for regulars."

When Victor was brought in, a courtesy call went to Arkady to come fish him from the tank. It was an arrangement some might call collusion. More and more Arkady found he was deviating from the straight and narrow.

"So Sergei Borodin came to be alone."

"Who said he came alone?"

Arkady was befuddled. "Why would a sober man bring anyone to a drunk tank?"

The medic inhaled hard enough to make his cigarette spark. "Sometimes I think the sexual revolution completely passed you by. If you think about it, it's an intimate situation, isn't it? The nudity. The dark. The beds."

It took forever for the coin to drop.

"Here?" Arkady had never considered the drunk tank right for an erotic rendezvous.

"It's ideal for rough trade, for a customer who likes a touch of squalor and a little risk."

"Who with?"

Swan went back through the log. Every other week or so, the names of Sergei Borodin and Roman Spiridon arrived and left together. The one time Borodin came alone was the night Spiridon stayed home, slipped into the bath and opened a vein.

Swan said, "I noticed old scars on Borodin's wrist. He'd tried to harm himself before. It's really a call for help, you know."

"You mean Spiridon's wrist."

"No, look in the log. Spiridon came here alone, got half the drunks here shouting they were God and went his merry way."

That was at the same time Roman Spiridon was slipping into his bathtub, Arkady thought. Two Spiridons, two separate places. It worked for electrons but not for any larger entity.

Arkady showed the medic the photograph he had taken from Madame Spiridona. "Who is this?"

"Borodin. Sergei Borodin."

Arkady took it back. Maybe there were two Borodins.

"How well do you know him?"

"Just from here. To be honest, I sometimes have trouble telling them apart."

"You never talked to him?"

"The usual. He was kind of sad and shy. A suicide is a suicide."

No, Arkady thought. In the proper hands, suicide was murder.

31

A male voice answered the phone.

"Hello. Who is this?"

"Anya's neighbor."

"Anya who?"

"The dead Anya, who else. Think about it. I'll call back in a minute. Talk to Mother."

Arkady hung up.

He took a bottle of vodka out of the refrigerator and poured it into a glass. When people used to propose a toast to world peace, his father would say, "I'm sick of toasting world peace. What about world war?" To the old son of a bitch.

Arkady drained the short glass in one go and let its warmth spread through him like water down a chandelier. He stood the bottle and glass on a counter.

He took ten minutes and called again.

This time the voice said, "Renko, what do you think you have?"

"A witness."

"Impossible."

"Why?" When there was no reply, Arkady said, "See? You can't deny it without admitting you were there."

"Where would that be?"

"Where 'God is shit.'"

A thoughtful pause. "Something can be arranged. Where are you?"

"I told you, I'm in the apartment across from hers. This will cost a hundred thousand dollars."

There was a whispered consultation at the other end. Sergei came back on the line and said, "I don't know what you're talking about. Stay there. I'll come by in three hours with at least a hundred thousand."

"Here in one hour." Arkady rang off.

It had sounded like Sergei was calling on a mobile phone. He was already on his way.

Arkady stood at the kitchen window. The sun lingered, a wan spectator to twilight. The road workers on his street had filled the pothole, again. They loaded their tar pot and compactor onto a truck and left the repair guarded by pylons with reflective stripes and a sign with the international symbol of a man digging, although on this detail all the crew were women. The crew supervisor was a man who seemed unfamiliar with a shovel. For his part, Arkady had taped one voice-activated recorder on the underside of the kitchen table and another recorder in the small of his back. At the end of the block, a black Hummer parked and took up the space of two ordinary cars. Sergei Borodin got out swinging a briefcase as if he hadn't a care in the world.

Arkady cracked the door. He heard footsteps climb the stairs until they reached the landing below.

"Renko?"

"Yes?"

"No emotions. We're all grown-ups. Just business, right?"

"Just business," Arkady agreed.

Out of his Petrouchka costume, Borodin looked like an average athlete in designer sweats, but Arkady recalled being impressed by Sergei's daring as he flew on wires in the Club Nijinsky. Physical courage Sergei had. What murderers usually lacked was empathy. He recalled Sergei sitting on a catwalk and dropping lit matches on the dancers below.

And what did Sergei see in Arkady besides a former investigator, bitter, cashiered and out of shape?

Arkady said, "Do you mind if we talk in the kitchen? At parties, people always end up in the kitchen." He kept Sergei in the corner of his eye as he led the way. "I want you to set the briefcase on the table. If there's a gun inside, and you don't tell me right now, I'll kill you."

"That's a joke?"

"No."

Sergei put the briefcase on the table and drew his hands back. "There's a gun inside."

"Thank you. I'm glad you told me. Push it over."

Sergei slid the case with his fingertips.

Arkady opened it and tucked the gun, a Makarov, under his belt. There was a newspaper for ballast. Nothing else. "You know, this is disappointing."

"Banks are closed. You gave me an hour. My money's tied up."

"In what?"

"What do you mean?"

"In what fields have you invested?"

"What do you care?"

"I have a stake in this too. When I was dismissed I was penalized half of my pension. Now you're my pension."

"Okay. People want me to do a martial arts film. East meets West, violence meets meditation and tons of 'wire fu.'"

"I remember. You're very good at flying on the wire, but you've killed at least one woman that I know of, probably more. What makes you think you'll be making movies?"

"You said that, not me. Besides, you're no hero yourself. They dismissed you."

"That's true."

Arkady turned his back on Sergei to pour two glasses of vodka. In the cabinet's reflection, he saw Sergei steal a look toward the door. Arkady filled a third glass and said, "Go ahead, ask her in. We don't want to leave Mother out."

"I came alone."

"Or I'll shoot you in the foot."

"Wait!"

There was no greater threat to a dancer.

Madame Borodina glided into the apartment, imperious and tanned, with little difference between her leather pants and jacket and her skin. Arkady thought she would have made a great pharaoh, the kind that demanded pyramids. He remembered two people had left Anya's apartment the night she was attacked. Madame Borodina he wouldn't turn his back on.

"Do you mind?" He spilled the contents of her evening bag onto the kitchen table: house and car keys, lady's compact, tissue, small bills, bank card, Metro pass and a .22-caliber pistol. He was uneasy. The Borodins might be amateurs, but they were not idiots. They followed orders but they weren't cowed.

Madame Borodina said, "Sergei, keep in mind that everything you say here is undoubtedly being recorded and that former investigator Renko is a desperate man ready to twist anything you say."

"Cheers," Arkady said.

They each drained their glass. Arkady felt warm. He didn't necessarily want the Borodins drunk. Loose and boastful would do. A little terror wouldn't hurt.

Madame Borodina said, "Now that you're not an investigator anymore, you will have to obey the law."

"Actually, you have it backward," Arkady said. "Now I don't."

"So who is this so-called witness?"

But Arkady slapped his forehead. "Sergei, I just realized what your film will be about. Not martial arts. Nijinsky! You will dance. You will play Nijinsky."

"I am Nijinsky."

Arkady raised his glass. "I'll drink to that."

Everyone had to drink to that. Arkady thought the tea party was going well. "So, if you play Nijinsky, who will play your mother? She was so dedicated. She picked his lovers, male or female, on the basis of whether they could promote his career. A lot of mothers wouldn't do that. Do you have anyone in mind?"

"You're funny," Sergei said.

"We're getting off the subject," Madame Borodina said. "I want to see this so-called witness."

Arkady said, "The subject is that Sergei didn't come with the money, he came with a gun. We have to work together." He refilled the glasses and, without explanation, added a fourth. "You were saying about Nijinsky's mother . . ."

Sergei laughed. "She was a controlling bitch."

"Sergei, don't play his game." Madame Borodina was not amused.

"So if you play Nijinsky, who will play the other women in your life? They must be difficult to cast."

"Very difficult," Sergei said.

"How many have you tried out?"

"Five." Sergei and his mother exchanged glances.

"Does she have to be a dancer?"

"Not if she has the right quality."

"They all fell short? Did they all turn out to be whores? What do you do to whores?"

"I don't understand."

"Did you expose them?" Arkady asked.

Madame Borodina told Sergei, "There is no witness. It's a hoax. Renko wants to extort money from innocent people."

Arkady had left it up to Anya when to make her appearance. Everything stopped as she entered the kitchen. She was paler than usual, which made the shadows under her eyes appear darker than ever, and she had taken care to dress in the cotton nightgown Sergei had seen her in last.

Sergei looked ready to burst from his skin. Arkady wondered if the family of Lazarus hadn't reacted with the same horror when he rose from the dead.

"Don't say anything," Madame Borodina said.

Sergei said, "When I left her she was blue!"

That was a start but not complete enough, Arkady thought.

"Shut up, Sergei!" Madame Borodina said.

Arkady said, "Sergei Borodin, did you try to murder the journalist Anya Rudikova?"

"I did." He added, "We can't help it. We're monsters."

"What do you mean?" This wasn't quite what Arkady had in mind.

"Have you noticed that Moscow is full of monsters?"

"What kind?" Arkady asked.

"All kinds. Don't you see them? They've been summoned."

"Sergei, please, I've heard all this," Madame Borodina said.

"Peter the Great had a museum of freaks, children with horns and hooves, the half formed and deformed. He sent out a decree that all such monsters in Russia be brought to him. It was called the 'Monster Decree.' It's happening again, only this time money rules. Monsters are gathering in Moscow. Whores, millionaires, like dung beetles rolling dollar bills. God is dog, Dog is shit, I am God." He turned to Anya and said, "If you're back from the dead, you are the greatest monster of all."

The room was silent.

"I killed them," Sergei finally said.

"How many?" Arkady pressed.

"Does it matter?"

Madame Borodina dragged Sergei away. "We're going. These crude theatrics will never stand up in court."

The Borodins retreated to the landing, but the stairs were blocked by Victor in work coveralls and reeking of tar.

32

Elsewhere horse racing was the sport of kings. In Russia it was the sport of the lower class. Workers used to come from nearby factories to catch the last half of the card. Now the factories were closed and the few who came were pensioners measuring vodka in plastic cups. The totalizator that stood on the infield was an antique. Losing tickets accumulated in drifts, food stalls were closed, urinals overflowed, devotees in the stands were all men and all of gray age. Yet they continued to bet. That, Arkady thought, said something about the human spirit.

If the sun shined on Moscow, it shined doubly on Sasha. He was a hero and a billionaire, an attractive combination. He liked to say, "He who steals my purse steals trash." It occurred to Arkady that Sasha had accumulated a lot of trash.

Today the Hippodrome felt Sasha's golden touch. Party tents were set up along the rail. Waitresses shuttled back and forth from catering trucks to the tents bearing champagne, salmon, grilled langoustines, for what was to all effects a club of millionaires with grease on their chins.

Senators, ministers and chief executives who would have avoided Sasha a week before were willing to accept Sasha's largesse now that he was back in the good graces of the Kremlin. He had his passport and a return ticket to the financial stratosphere. The table chatter was intense, interrupted only every twenty minutes or so by a horse race. Pacers and trotters.

Although the day was clear, the track was slop. Mud exploded under the horses, drivers cracked their whips and drove blindly, goggles caked with mud, urging their horses, "Come on, you fucking cow," while over the PA system, the recorded sound of cheering crowds poured over the nearly empty stands.

Arkady nursed his hangover in the umbra of red velvet curtains. Petals of plaster fell on his shoulders from a ceiling mural that incorporated horses, hammers and sickles. Folding chairs huddled under a plastic sheet. A mini-refrigerator was unplugged and empty.

His eye fell on a thrown-away bet. It took a moment for his brain to kick in. He took an envelope from his jacket, and tapped out the half ticket he found in the trunk of the Mercedes. The two tickets were printed on the same cheap paper, but the ticket from the floor had a complete name: *Central Moscow Hippodrome,* and was stamped from the Sunday before.

He called Victor.

"The ticket is from the Hippodrome. Not the circus, not a film. I don't know whether Dopey played the horses, but the crowds out here have been getting sparse and a dwarf would stand out."

"You're there now?" Victor asked.

"In the royal box."

"You've moved up in the world."

Sasha Vaksberg spotted Arkady. He looked puzzled but put on a big smile and waved.

Looking down at the tents, Arkady was impressed by how quickly Sasha had mustered his troops of caterers, waiters and bodyguards. He should feel good, Arkady thought, like Napoleon returning from Elba.

The luncheon seemed to take forever. Finally, there was a last bear hug and a last guest to push out the door. The caterers began clearing tables and breaking down the tents and buffets. After a flurry of mobile phone calls, Sasha held up a bottle of champagne and waved Arkady to come down to the rail. Vaksberg was exuberant.

"You should have joined the party and let them see us together. I get blessed by the pope, you get blessed by the cardinal. That's the way it works." Sasha caught his breath. "The place is a miracle. You know the rationale for its existence? Horses for the cavalry. In a nuclear war, we'll all be issued sabers and a horse."

"I take it you're launching a new venture?"

"Looking for investors, yes. This is the way it's done. Money attracts money. And they all love being with a hero."

"That's you?"

"That's me now. Have some champagne, for Lord's sake."

"Is it good?"

"These people expect the best. They have built their dacha, own a town house in London, an island in the Caribbean and a private jet to take them there and they still can't spend it fast enough. They ski, sail, buy a football or basketball team and still can't spend it fast enough. The answer is obvious. Own a racehorse. Better yet, own a stable of racehorses."

"Horse racing is for the working class."

"That's harness racing. We have to drive home the idea that

there's nothing more prestigious than losing money on your own string of Thoroughbred horses."

A blast of patriotic music on the PA system announced the last race of the day. The crowd was male, largely pensioners who gathered every Sunday during the racing season to study the form. The most serious were known as the Faculty. They could not lose a fortune, because the largest bet allowed was ten rubles. Play money. Arkady wondered why they didn't just watch ants at an anthill.

"Is this your next project?"

"It might be," Vaksberg said. "I'm back in the game, that's the main thing. By the way, where is Anya? It's been days since she called. She said she'd be staying with a friend. She doesn't answer her cell phone and she didn't leave a number."

"I suppose when she wants to get hold of you, she will."

Sasha said, "My relationship with Anya is complicated. Has she told you that she has a contract to do a book on me? It's her great chance and she is an ambitious girl. And she may have some confidential internal company papers and I may have to sue her to keep her from publishing, but that's down the line. The main thing is I own her. Did she tell you that?"

They were interrupted by a call on Arkady's phone. It was Victor.

"Your Dopey is, or was, Pavel Petrovich Maksimov, thirty-two, resident of Moscow, never missed a day at the track unless he was in jail. Everyone at the Hippodrome will know him."

"Present employment?"

"Legitimate? He ran the 'Whack-a-Mole' concession in Gorky Park. Let's assume that he was dealing drugs. Before that, he was a croupier at the Peter the Great Casino at Three Stations. He must have had a hell of a long rake."

Arkady hung up. There was silence in the royal box until

Sasha said, "Ask around all you want. Criminals in Moscow casinos? What a shocker."

The last race got off to a rolling start behind a gate truck that folded its ungainly wings on the run. Six trotters followed, running stiffly on in their traces, unnatural and beautiful. On the PA system the world cheered.

"I gave you too much credit, Renko. I took you for a man of the world. What you call skimming was a normal transfer of funds within different parts of a corporation. I can see why someone who is not from the business world might misinterpret some transactions. It will all be repaid with interest, no harm done."

"You skimmed ninety percent off a fund for children."

"Totally legal. A luxury fair is an expensive, complicated operation. I did create a reserve fund for unexpected costs. It's normal business practice. In other words, we can tie you up in the courts forever and sue you for libel to boot. Look, I'll be honest with you. It was going to be a simple robbery. Maksimov and I agreed there wouldn't be any shooting. I admit I underestimated the little bastard's greed, but we have to move on. It's your word against mine. Renko's word against mine. I never pulled a trigger."

"That's not what you told the police," Arkady reminded him. "You can't change your story now. You're a hero."

33

Since Emma was the youngest member of the family, she was given the job of finding the baby a new home. She could leave it in a park, a box, a bench, a public toilet, anywhere as long as she didn't involve the police.

"What about Itsy?" Emma pulled on her jacket inch by inch.

Klim was taking over. He said, "She's dead. And Tito and Leo and Peter. You're lucky you're not dead too. Just dump the baby and do it fast before it wakes up."

"She has one more bottle of formula."

"So?"

"What if nobody finds her?"

"Then she's out of luck."

The way people talked about luck, it sounded to Emma like a spoonful of water in the desert. There just wasn't enough to go around.

But as she made her way through the cars parked in front of Kazansky Station, she came upon a huge sedan with a rear door open to a leather seat as soft as a mother's lap. Emma slid the baby in and it looked so peaceful that Emma laid her own head down for just a second. The next thing Emma knew, she was waking up in the rear seat and a woman behind the wheel was shouting, "Get out! Get out, you filthy girl!"

Dizzy and exhausted, Emma wanted to join Klim and the others. The problem was that the underground passage to the other side of Three Stations was blocked by a scuffle between skinheads and Tajiks. She had been uneasy about her mission from the beginning and it wasn't all that easy to leave a baby. She had expected to prop the baby up in a trash basket where it would be seen and rescued and all she could find were plastic modules for the collection of recyclables—green for paper goods and blue for plastics and glass. She didn't want people throwing empty bottles on the baby. Most of the traffic was speeding through the square. A yellow Volvo station wagon trolled around the parked cars and came to a halt in front of Emma and the baby. A Gypsy with a baby at her breast stopped alongside Emma. The car moved on.

The baby stretched and pursed its lips and made all the signs usual to waking and crying. Emma felt she had to take cover soon, and when traffic passed, the empty street lured her out. She was halfway across when the next wave of cars caught up. It was like stepping into the sea up to her neck, the cars so huge and black and their lights so blinding that Emma dropped the baby. It was just too heavy and floppy. But when she remembered that Itsy never abandoned anyone, she rushed back to cover the baby with her own body even as the lights of a flatbed truck rose over her. The truck shuddered to a stop amid the explosive popping of straps and the release of a plastic tarp that lifted like a great bat ray. Two men climbed down from the cab, faces white with anxiety. All traffic had stopped. Their load of exotic mammoth tusks was strewn over four lanes and stopped traffic as effectively as tank traps. The tusks represented months of trekking across Siberian permafrost, power-hosing tusk after tusk to bring back collector-quality finds, hand sawing the final lot in a Moscow bathtub.

The driver got down on one knee to look under his truck. And then shot to his feet.

"Little fucks, where are you?"

Emma was already squirming between cars and making her exit, heading toward the statue of Lenin alongside Kazansky Station. The baby was crying at the top of her lungs.

No one was there. She had no money, no friends and nowhere to put the baby. Around her, she saw nothing but ominous shadows and heard nothing but curses and blows of men fighting for possession of a doorway.

The baby was a fire siren, and there was nothing Emma could do to comfort her. She pulled out her final bottle of premixed formula. One arm around the baby, she tried to open the bottle. It danced perversely on her fingertips, fell, and shattered. Scavengers approached to see if there was anything worth stealing. Hands snatched her bag and ran off with it.

An old woman in a cape asked, "Boy or girl?"

The baby was so startled by the woman's appearance she was momentarily silent.

"Girl," Emma got out.

"Excellent choice. Have you ever seen a piece of bread make it to the bottom of a pond?"

"No."

"That's right, because things that sink to the bottom of a pond get eaten. I've been watching you."

"Where?"

"From up there." She pointed to an apartment building that rose at the end of the Kazansky Station grounds.

"How can you see in the dark?"

"I'll show you. That baby shouldn't be out in the rain."

"It's a warm rain."

"Maybe God's pissing on us. Ready?"

"Thank you." Emma remembered her manners.

"You can call me Madame Furtseva, although Madame will do."

Madame Furtseva was the closest thing to a witch Emma had ever met. Also, she believed in rice. She made rice water for the baby and rice pudding for the girl. As Emma ate she gawked at the variety of photographs, artifacts and souvenirs from around the world. And Madame Furtseva did not ask questions, although she knew a great deal.

"I can't get to water holes in Africa anymore, so I photograph the water holes that are here. It's not so different. There are lions and buffalo and jackals, many jackals. I take pictures of them using an infrared filter. They can't see me but I can see them."

Madame Furtseva opened a portfolio and showed Emma a landscape of pink trees under a dark sky, a portrait of milky round-faced Yegor and a group of girls running with a dog. Motion swirled around them.

"Itsy and Tito and Milka and me."

She looked at that one a long time.

34

Arkady felt as though he were in a small boat on a large sea. Great struggles took place far below on the ocean bottom, creating waves on the surface and casting up myriad strange creatures. The how or why he didn't know. Everything powerful was hidden. Every order was silent. Why had he been given his gun back? Those who knew, knew.

Traffic on Mira usually crawled, but at this time of night, cars were bold and loud. A roar ran along the front of the Agricultural Ministry, not the whisper of a Mercedes but the wild tones of the Maserati and Ferrari.

Traffic police stood helplessly by their police-issue Ladas. Giving chase to a Porsche or BMW ended up as a sobering demonstration of how outclassed they were. Audis and hypertuned Mazdas came in waves like surfers. They had raced, illegally, around the Peripheral Road. Downtown Moscow was their victory lap.

When Arkady felt the nudge from behind, he took it as a

cue to get out of the way. He was already at the speed limit and the Lada was beginning to sound like a biplane. He let a black Hummer go by and ventured out onto the Boulevard Ring. Upscale then, upscale now. A smooth ride by the House of Music. And then a nudge from behind again, this time harder. Another Hummer. Or the same one. Arkady couldn't see the driver because the windshield was tinted. The front end had high chrome bumpers. When Arkady tried to stop, the Hummer pushed the Lada along. He shifted to neutral before the gearbox broke.

Arkady felt around for his sacred blue roof light, his safe passage to the city. It was usually on the dash. Not now. The Lada's temporary door did not lock. Someone had just reached in and plucked the light like an apple on a low-hanging branch. The Hummer shoveled the Lada along, and a trickle of sweat moved down the back of his neck. If he could only see who was driving, he could get some grasp of what he was contending with. Before he knew it, they were in a tunnel, and the air imploded. As they emerged, a Hitachi sign greeted them. Illuminated panels extolled the beaches of Orlando, Florida, spearfishing in the Red Sea, swimming in the turquoise waters of Croatia, places he'd love to go to if he could get untangled from the car behind him. A straightaway along the Kremlin wall. Not a single guard. Wasn't anyone protecting our leaders? Finally, blessed centrifugal force. At the bottom of the Alexander Garden, the Lada made a tighter turn and slid off the Hummer's bumper. Arkady put the car into third gear as two hubcaps rolled freely alongside.

Traffic police in shiny slickers waved Arkady to a stop. For the first time in his life he was happy to see them.

"You don't deny you were racing?"

"I wasn't racing; I was running for my life."

"Racing or running, that's going to cost you five hundred rubles. And your car, we'll have to confiscate your car." The officer took a good look at it. "You have to take your car."

The second officer said, "We'll take five dollars."

"I was escaping from . . ." Arkady looked around. There was no sign of the Hummer.

Arkady's cell phone rang inside the Lada. Each move he made, the officers blocked his way.

"Oh no, pay up first."

"I need to answer the phone."

"Money first."

"I'm a senior investigator."

"Show me your papers."

Five dollars proved to be papers enough.

But the ringing had stopped. There was only a message from Victor.

"You're not going to believe this. That bastard, your former boss Prosecutor Zurin, says that since you were dismissed, nothing on the tape is admissible as evidence. That includes confessions gained by 'cheap theatrics.' He says it is nothing but the rant of a sick individual."

Arkady tried to call back but Victor's phone was already engaged. And he tried to reach Anya's cell phone because if the Borodins were loose they would have a chance to kill her a second time, which seemed unfair. There was no answer.

What was the story about an appointment in Samarra? Arkady thought. Trying to avoid death, we run into its arms. It was unavoidable, at this traffic light or the next.

And there it was, pulling in snug behind Arkady, a black Hummer with a blue light—most likely Arkady's—riding on its roof. On the first blink of the traffic light, Arkady made a U-turn into oncoming traffic. The Hummer followed but was too large to thread the needle cleanly. It clipped fenders as it forced its way but followed in Arkady's tracks. What had his father said? "In the field, an officer should run only as a last resort." This wasn't retreat, this was panic. Arkady took a full turn at the round-about at Lubyanka Square heading for narrow streets with side-walk cafés. He leaned on the horn and got a feeble *bleat*. Cafés were shutting down. A tower of stacked chairs tottered and fell. Somewhere along the line, the Lada's wing mirrors had disap-peared, and he had to look in the rearview mirror. The Hummer had a police beam, and in its glare, Arkady could barely see. It didn't matter, they were in his neighborhood now.

Arkady floored the knob that was all that remained of Vic-tor's accelerator. The Lada started to shake apart. The exhaust pipe dragged, playing a tune on the surface of the road. The Hummer tried to pass. Arkady kept the Lada's nose in front. With one block to go, the Hummer pulled alongside. The driver rolled his window down. Sergei was at the wheel. His mother sat beside him. Mother and son, a family portrait, Arkady thought. He steered a little closer and Sergei corrected, allow-ing the Lada to keep its nose ahead. White smoke spewed from under the hood.

Sergei pointed a gun at Arkady. Arkady aimed his pistol, the gift of the Russian people, in return. Madame Borodina was shouting, although Arkady could not make out the words. He cut the wheel and leaned into the Hummer, toward an orange pylon lying on its side.

"I am God!" Sergei shouted.

The Hummer hit the pothole at 150 kph.

Neither Borodin was belted. Both burst through the wind-shield as the Hummer stood on its head and made a pirouette in midair before it landed.

35

He followed Arkady onto a little green commuter train, the sort that minds its own business and noses its way from big city stations to the bare platforms of villages. Seats were wooden and made for discomfort. It was hard enough for him to move. He accepted the pain as punishment for having botched the job.

Tajiks! Why hadn't anyone informed them that the shed was a Tajik heroin depot? They would have made arrangements. Instead, his brother is mauled by the fucking hound from hell. Abandoning Ilya had been the hardest decision of his life, but it wasn't as though he had a choice, not with a bullet through his shoulder and some Asiatic rifleman aching to put him in the crosshairs again. Took him three hours to crawl to the door. The episode was shameful and only fueled his determination to make things right.

It had taken two weeks to heal up but the time had not been wasted. He took the commuter train that Renko used morning and evening now that he was reinstated at the prosecutor's office. At first he sat at the far end of the car just to test the water and make himself familiar. He took note of what book Renko was reading and bought a copy of another book by the same author. The book was pure bullshit but he understood the themes. A day later, he was already discussing the books with him.

Renko was such a fraud. Security at the prosecutor's office was a fraud too. He had shown up in the uniform of a deliveryman with a package that absolutely, positively had to reach Arkady Renko. He got the city and country address. He had the goods on Renko, who had everyone fooled. A choirboy, except real choirboys didn't shoot people.

He took precautions. Cut and dyed his hair gray, inserted steel caps on his front teeth. Those were the two features that people noticed most. Hair and teeth.

They walked part of the way to the village together. He had taken a room at a local farmhouse for a pittance in cash. His story was that he had high blood pressure and his doctor had advised him to go somewhere with fresh air and springwater. A rest in the country was the best medicine. Renko pointed out a pond just large enough to justify a rowboat and a plastic kayak that lazed upside down at a dock. He almost overstepped when he told Renko the pond was little bigger than a piss hole, then began dropping hints that a dip in it would be a capper to his vacation. He didn't push too hard or too soon because the girl might recognize him.

There were four in Renko's party. He would have to get them all in one fell swoop. But he liked this kind of problem. He liked the puzzle about a goat, a chicken and a fox crossing a river in a boat. There were things to take into consideration, like time of day and greatest surprise. He would have to eliminate Renko first, then the boy and women. That would mean getting Renko alone.

The village had a shop that sold used farm tools on consignment. He bought a spade, a scythe and a whetstone. Just swinging the scythe and listening to its whistle made him feel more grounded. He grew to hate the long conversations on the train, the forced bonhomie. His face hurt from grinning.

There was a deadline. Renko had confided that they would be going back to the city at the week's end. He scouted Renko's dacha. There were hazards in that. He was almost spotted by a suspicious neighbor. And there was a party at Renko's that he was invited to. He begged off in case it was a trap, but watched through binoculars. Renko said he shouldn't be so shy.

Arkady spotted him the minute he was on the train. He was a jackal trying to hide among lapdogs. He had blunt, half-finished features with a heavy brow and large, capable hands. The newcomer said his name was Yakov Lozovsky, an engineer from Moscow vacationing on his own. Arkady ran "Yakov Lozovsky" through the files and found that, indeed, there was an engineer by that name and he was on vacation. Nevertheless, Arkady began carrying his pistol, and Victor came to add an extra body.

Arkady was on paid leave. There had been no formal ceremony of reinstatement, only a summons to the office of Assistant Deputy Gendler. Ever since he had been reinstated, Zurin had treated his investigator with great consideration, as if they were both struggling toward the "Truth," each in his own way. Zurin got most of the credit for outwitting and stopping a serial killer, which was only his due as a senior officer.

The issue was whether to stay at the dacha or return to the city. To break routine might be more dangerous than retreat. Maya called him the Catcher and said he would never stop. She would always live in fear. Anya said she had already been dead, she had nothing to lose. Zhenya was eager to be a protector in Maya's eyes. Arkady warned that they would have to do without cell phones because there was no coverage at the dacha, no landline and help too far away in any case.

They could feel the Catcher prowling in the dark. In any

siege, success was a matter of patience. Yakov Lozovsky had a clean record and was not breaking any laws, yet fear set in, evidenced by contrary bouts of claustrophobia and a reluctance to leave the house. Anya was sharp with Arkady during the day. At night, in bed, she pressed herself against his back and clung for reassurance.

Only Maya and Zhenya were home when Yakov showed up with an ax at the back door of the dacha. He had the broad physique of someone who had done manual labor all his life. He had taken off his shirt to chop wood and the bullet scar on his shoulder was a raw welt. Maya shrank into a corner out of sight.

"Who's home?"

"People are around," Zhenya said. He couldn't control his trembling. He remembered Yakov riding a battered station wagon and waving a reward poster for Maya.

"Around what?"

"They're around."

"Now, here's the question. Do you need any firewood?"

"No, thanks," said Zhenya.

"It's no problem." Yakov pointed to the logs stacked outside the back door. He picked up the largest piece of wood, set it on a stump, and split it with the ax. Like a man snapping a toothpick. "It won't take a second. No one will know I was even here. No? You're sure?"

"I'm sure," Zhenya said.

"Well, only trying to help. It's going to rain tonight. Good for the farmers."

As soon as Yakov got back to the farmhouse, he sketched an outline of the dacha, all the access points, the windows and doors and chimney, driveway, dock, fields of vision. Then he sat back and waited for rain.

The rain was perfect, a steady downpour with no lightning.

A friend of Renko's watched from a Lada at the front door. It didn't matter. The man who called himself Yakov Lozovsky swam across the pond to the least defended side of the dacha. In his wet suit, he was virtually invisible. All he carried was a waterproof sack containing two smoke grenades and a ballistic gas mask with huge eyes and a silicone seal. In a leg sheath was a SAS fighting knife, good for slashing as well as sticking. He watched from the vantage point between the rowboat and the kayak as lamps went out in the dacha one by one. As the last lamp was doused and Yakov slowly rose from the water, the rowboat flipped and he was slit open from his sternum to his balls.

Arkady pitched himself backward as an effusion of warmth spread through the water. A hand clutched his ankle. He kicked free but lost his knife and backpedaled to deeper water, where standing upright on the spongy bottom of the pond was a balancing act. Holding his skin together like a vest, Yakov got a handhold on Arkady's belt and embraced him from behind. There was a little jiggle; that would be Yakov drawing a knife, Arkady thought. The man unraveled, yet here he was, a professional, carrying on. Arkady heard Victor shout from the front of the house, too far away to help. Zhenya jumped in from the dock but he could barely swim.

What distracted the man was the sight of Maya in the glow of a lantern at the edge of the pond. Here was the child whore he had been chasing almost in his grasp. Her lantern shined and laid a golden path across the surface of the water. All he had to do was follow the reflection.

Arkady ducked out of the man's grip and dove. From the bottom of the pond, he looked up at a silhouette of Yakov turning left and right in a cloud of blood.

Arkady surfaced long enough to say, "Are you the last one?" He dove before Yakov could strike.

"Will they send anyone else?" Arkady surfaced in a different direction.

"Who are you?"

But the man who called himself Yakov Lozovsky died like a scorpion, spinning and stabbing the water.

36

A stage was set up where the trailer had been. The acts were simple: marionettes, trained dogs, a sword swallower, a juggler and a monkey who collected money in a cap. Although the cap was shabby and the monkey had the mange, an outdoor circus on a sunny day drew young families that usually avoided Three Stations.

To add to the holiday air, the piano from the Yaroslavl Station waiting room had been brought outside. For all the times Arkady had come in and out of the station, he had never heard the piano being played. Someone was playing it now, despite the fact that the piano had not been tuned in years. Unexpected sharps and flats abounded, and some keys were totally dead.

In short, Arkady thought, Russia set to music.

Some men chase butterflies; others let butterflies come to them. Arkady stayed by the circus while Maya and Anya ran after every stroller and Zhenya and Victor patrolled the sidewalk. Maya's hair was growing back but she was frail and drawn from weeks of search.

Arkady noticed that a little girl with a baby in her arms was taking in more money than the monkey. It bared its teeth at her and she shrieked.

"Does he bite?" she asked no one in particular.

"Well, he's sulking at the moment. He's embarrassed about his cap."

"Is he really? How can you tell?"

"Look at him, downcast eyes, runny nose. He's in a state."

"I like dogs. I had a friend who had a dog. Tito."

"Good dog?"

"The best." She started to tear and caught herself. "I'm with Madame now but she can't come out because of the sun."

"That's a pretty blue blanket. What's the baby's name?" Arkady asked.

She hesitated in her snuffling.

He asked, "Is it Katya?"

"I'm just taking care of the baby until her mother comes."

"I can see what a good job you're doing. It's a big responsibility."

"Who are you? Are you a magician?"

Arkady said, "Kind of. I can't make rabbits pop out of hats. That's not useful anyway; people don't have room for rabbits. First you have two, then you have twenty. I'm more useful. I know things."

"Like what?"

"I know that the baby's blanket has a pattern of ducklings."

"That doesn't prove anything. You could have peeked."

"And if you lift the hair on the back of her head, there's a birthmark in the shape of a question mark."

"Is not."

"Look and see."

She shifted the baby to examine the back of her neck. When she saw the mark, her jaw fell open.

"How did you know?"

"First, I'm a magician and second, I know Katya's mommy. She's been looking for Katya for weeks."

"I didn't steal her."

"I know that."

Emma teared up again. "What do I do?"

"Very simple. Take Katya over to her mommy and say, 'I found your baby.' There she is." Arkady pointed out Maya at the circus entrance. With her short hair she wasn't difficult to spot.

Emma said, "She's just a girl."

"That's enough."

The monkey tried to drag Emma back toward the ring, where dogs were performing, jumping over each other like a self-shuffling deck of cards. Emma tried to shake the monkey off. Arkady lured it away with a five-ruble note. He watched Emma's tentative progress around a clown with a red nose, blowing bubbles. Past an acrobat on stilts, who took slow-motion strides. Past children of seesaw age queuing at a miniature roller coaster and past older kids tossing quoits. And through a maze of strollers, to the moment when Maya looked up and light leapt into her eyes.

Acknowledgments

I am always amazed by the fact that intelligent people with better things to do offer me their time and expertise. They include, in Moscow; Colonel Alexander Yakovlev, detective; Lyuba Vinogradova, assistant and interpreter; Yegor Tolstyakov, editor and advisor; journalist Lana Kapriznaya; Oksana Dribas of the Club Diaghilev; Alexander Nurnberg, journalist; Boris Rudenko, writer; Andrei Sychev, casino manager; Maxim Nenarokomov, art critic, and Samuel Kip Smith, assistant. Natalia Drozdova and Natalia Snournikova of the "Otradnoye" children's shelter have my admiration and thanks.

Doctors Neal Benowitz, Nelson Branco, Mark Levy, Ken Sack and Michael Weiner attempted to explain the physical world to me. Don Sanders, Luisa Cruz Smith and Ellen Branco offered insight and support.

Finally, I thank Christian Rohr and David Rosenthal for their limitless patience, and Andrew Nurnberg and the late Knox Burger for a few million things.

About the Author

Martin Cruz Smith's novels include *Gorky Park, Stallion Gate, Polar Star, December 6,* and *Stalin's Ghost*. A two-time winner of the Hammett Prize from the International Association of Crime Writers and a recipient of Britain's Golden Dagger Award, he lives in California.